THE
DURANGO STAGE

Center Point
Large Print

Also by Wayne D. Overholser and available from Center Point Large Print:

Black Mike
Gunlock
Twin Rocks

**This Large Print Book carries the
Seal of Approval of N.A.V.H.**

THE
DURANGO STAGE

A Western Trio

WAYNE D.
OVERHOLSER

CENTER POINT LARGE PRINT
THORNDIKE, MAINE

The text of this Large Print edition is unabridged.
In other aspects, this book may vary from the original edition.
Printed in the United States of America on permanent paper.
Set in 16-point Times New Roman type.

ISBN: 978-1-62899-529-9 (hardcover)
ISBN: 978-1-62899-534-3 (paperback)

Library of Congress Cataloging-in-Publication Data

Overholser, Wayne D., 1906–1996.
[Short stories. Selections]
The Durango stage : a western trio / Wayne D. Overholser. —
    Center Point Large Print edition.
pages cm
Summary: "In three western stories, a man must use his wits to overcome what appears to be impossible situations"—Provided by publisher.
ISBN 978-1-62899-529-9 (hardcover : alk. paper)
ISBN 978-1-62899-534-3 (pbk. : alk. paper)
1. Large type books.
    I. Overholser, Wayne D., 1906–1996. Grangers, get your guns!
    II. Overholser, Wayne D., 1906–1996. It's hell to be a hero!
    III. Overholser, Wayne D., 1906–1996. Durango stage. IV. Title.
PS3529.V33A6 2015
813′.54—dc23
                                                    2014049683

TABLE OF CONTENTS

GRANGERS, GET YOUR GUNS!

I

Ed Rawlins carried a sack of flour out of the Mercantile, dumped it into his wagon, and straightened his lank body, looked across the street squarely into the eyes of Bal Tilse. It had been a long time since he'd seen Tilse. He rutted back into his memory. Five years . . . ? No, six—and he'd have been happier if it had been another six. His first impulse was to run, an impulse that died the instant it was born, for Ed Rawlins was not one to duck an issue.

It was not that he had anything against Tilse, for at one time the man had been his best friend. It was simply a case of Rawlins's smoky past being brought back to him in the form of Bal Tilse, a past that ran through the years like a frayed and tarnished ribbon. Rawlins, watching Tilse cross the street to him, thought grimly that Tilse was the last man he wanted to see. He thought, too, with a sharp stab of regret, that a man's past is always with him, always haunting him and casting its long shadow across his future.

"Ed, you old, long-legged, smoke-eating son of sin!" Tilse shouted, and held out a hand. "Sure is good to see you."

7

"It's good to see you," Rawlins lied, and shook Tilse's hand. "What are you doing here in Sills City?"

"Looking for a job . . . and for you. Heard you were here."

"You get a job?" Rawlins asked, and felt his stomach muscles knot. There was only one man in Sills City who would hire a gunslinger like Bal Tilse, and Rawlins knew the answer to his question before he asked it.

Tilse nodded. "Hired out to Ira Sills."

"Yeah, I know him," Rawlins murmured, and let it go at that.

Tilse cuffed his Stetson back, and stared at Rawlins, and Rawlins felt the disappointment and then the contempt that was in the man.

"You look like a farmer," Tilse said. "That don't make sense for a gent who had the fastest gun hand of any *hombre* I ever sided in a showdown."

"It doesn't make sense for a fact," agreed Rawlins mildly.

There was silence for a moment, both thinking of the years they had been together, and of that last ride through the blackness of an Arizona night with a dozen men not more than a jump behind them. They had parted in the desert while the pursuit thundered on past, and Rawlins had not heard of Tilse from that moment to this. Now, clad in the heavy shoes, the overalls, cotton work shirt, and straw hat of a farmer, Rawlins felt suddenly ashamed.

"It's damned funny," Tilse said, his green eyes narrowing. "I remember how I used to cuss a gunfighter's life, claiming I'd like to settle down on a farm and watch things grow. And all the time you said I was a damned fool."

"I was a crazy kid," Rawlins murmured, "and you were old enough to know what you wanted."

"And now you're digging in the dirt, and I'm still drawing down gunslinger's pay." Tilse shook his head as if he couldn't believe this thing he saw.

"I'm just one of fifty farmers, Bal," Rawlins said, "who settled here on Purgatory Creek and took land under Sills's ditch. I'd like to remain that."

"Hell, you got nothing to be ashamed of," Tilse said sharply. "No use hiding your talents." He paused, eyes again narrowing thoughtfully, as if his mind was trying to probe the mystery of this change in Rawlins. Bitterness came to him then. "I've been the fool, Ed, keeping on the dark trails half the time and wasting my life. I'm forty. Damned near ready to be an old man."

"I'm not so young, either, Bal. Well, I'll see you again."

Rawlins crawled into the wagon seat and picked up the lines. Tilse stared up at him, eyes still questioning. He asked softly: "You say this is Sills's land?"

Rawlins nodded. "State got it from the government under the Carey Act, and Sills had to put water on it."

"You get it free?"

'Not quite." Rawlins's lips tightened. "Fifteen dollars an acre."

"What the hell does he need gunslingers for?" Tilse demanded. "I figured he was having a scrap over water rights."

"No."

Tilse laid his hands on the front wheel, the sourness in him whetting an edge to his words. "I sure need a job, Ed, but I didn't figure that coming here would put us on opposite sides."

"Funny thing," Rawlins said, and clucked to his team.

Bal Tilse stood there in the street, staring after him, dark face still sour and a little puzzled.

It was strange what a man would do for a dream, Ed Rawlins told himself as he drove home. He thought now about his smoky years as he had not thought about them for a long time: empty years, filled with riding and shooting and killing, years when he'd earned big pay and spent it as fast as he'd earned it. Then there had been another job after he'd left Tilse, and another fight, and he'd been shot to pieces. It had been the weeks in a hospital bed that had changed him. He hadn't buckled on his guns since that time, hadn't fought with a man since then. He'd worked, and saved his money, and now he was making a try for his own land here on the Purgatory.

It wasn't the land, exactly, that was his dream.

He drove into his farmyard and past the house to his barn, looking at the buildings, critically now, and weighing them against the possessions that Bal Tilse's life had brought him. They weren't much: the house was a one-room, tar-paper shack; the barn was made of pine logs he'd brought down from the Cascades; his garden was just coming up and was nothing but a promise. He thought grimly of that. A promise? Nothing more and, unless Sills fixed the ditches so that he'd have more water than he'd had last year, it was a promise that would not be kept.

Rawlins put away his team, carried his groceries into the house, and cooked dinner, but his mind was still on the past, still considering the forces that had made him what he was. It was partly the pain and nearness to death while he'd been in the hospital, but it was mostly Trudy Gilder, and what she meant to him. That was the dream: her love, a home, children. Those were the things that gave a solitude to life, a feeling of depth, a value to the bare struggle of living. And Trudy Gilder did not approve of fighting. She would give him back his ring if she knew what his past had been. Shock came to Rawlins with that thought. If Tilse told, and the story spread along Purgatory Creek, Trudy would hear.

Ed Rawlins was not a man to give way to panic. He fought it now, telling himself it wouldn't happen, that Tilse wouldn't tell. Yet he couldn't be sure, and the worry was still in him that afternoon when he was working on his mower and saw Jack Kelton and Lew Dosso ride in from the county road.

At first the sight of Ira Sills's two men did not mean anything to Rawlins. He straightened, laid the monkey wrench on the mower seat, and reached into his pocket for pipe and tobacco. He called an amiable: "Howdy, gents! Light down and rest your saddles."

They dismounted, and came toward him, neither speaking and both, he saw, were a little drunk. Officially they were supposed to be some kind of construction men for the irrigation company but Rawlins, who understood these things better than most of the folks along the Purgatory, knew that their real job was to smash opposition to Sills. Kelton was a big, thick-shouldered man with sharp, black eyes that were surprisingly small for so large a face. Dosso was thin and stooped, with a huge beak of a nose and long-fingered hands that were deadly fast with the six-guns he wore. They made a good pair for Ira Sills and were the principal reason why none of the farmers had seriously kicked about the small and inadequate ditch system.

Rawlins wondered why neither spoke, but he didn't see their intent until they were close and Kelton said: "We thought you were just a farmer, Rawlins . . . just a plain, ordinary, mud farmer."

Bal Tilse had wasted no time about his past. That was the first thought that came into Rawlins's mind as he slid the tobacco can back into his pocket and held a match to his pipe. Then a second thought struck him: this was trouble with a capital T and he wished his guns were on his hips instead of in the house. "That's all I am," Rawlins said coolly, taking the pipe out of his mouth. "Just a farmer." He wondered why he'd thought about his guns and, remembering Trudy Gilder, knew he must meet this threat without his guns.

"I hear different," Kelton said. "I hear you used to be a gunfighter, a regular ring-tailed wowser. A real curly wolf from the forks of Bitter Crick."

"Who have you been listening to?" Rawlins asked.

"Don't make no never mind about that," Kelton snarled. "The point is, we don't want no trouble. You take fifty crazy mud farmers, get 'em heated up some, and you've got trouble. We ain't gonna have that, Rawlins."

"All right," Rawlins said, "we ain't gonna have trouble."

Lew Dosso had cocked his head, hard blue eyes on Rawlins. He said: "He could be a tough hand, Jack. Look at them gray eyes. And them long fingers. That quick way he's got of moving. Put a gun on his hip, and he could be hell on little red wheels."

"Rawlins, it don't make no sense for a gent who's been a gunslinger to come here and take up land and act like a farmer." Kelton gestured with a meaty hand. "You're playing some kind of smart game. What is it?"

Rawlins's pipe had gone dead in his mouth. He tamped the tobacco down with a forefinger, eyes on Kelton and then Dosso, and held a match flame to it. He knew men like these two, knew that the only things they respected were a man's fists or the gun he carried. He blew out a cloud of smoke that hung for a moment in the still air. Then he said: "To hell with you. There's no smart game about it. I want to farm and be let alone. That's all."

But Jack Kelton had not ridden out here from Sills City to let him alone. He snarled: "I think you're taking the farmers' pay, and, when the time's right, you'll buckle on your hog-legs and start raising hell."

"I haven't worn my guns for a long time, Kelton. Now suppose you mount up and git."

"Not yet, mister. I came out here to show you you'd better stay a farmer. Now I'm gonna show you."

Kelton lowered his head and came at Rawlins, great fists lashing out at Rawlins's face. It might have surprised a man who had less understanding of the caliber of those with whom he was dealing, but it did not surprise Ed Rawlins.

14

He had laid his pipe down on the mower seat beside the monkey wrench. Now he stepped to one side, and struck Kelton a jarring blow on the side of his head.

Kelton let out a bellow that held more surprise than pain, wheeled, and rushed Rawlins again. This time Rawlins held his ground. They came together, hard, Rawlins punching savagely at Kelton's stomach, but weight was with Kelton, and he forced Rawlins back. They moved toward the mower, Kelton lashing at Rawlins's face. Rawlins, seeing that it was Kelton's intention to back him against it and batter him into submission, suddenly swung away and brought a vicious right to the side of the man's face. Kelton went on, carried by his own impetus and the force of Rawlins's blow, and fell headlong against the mower, his head cracking sharply against the wheel.

Rawlins stepped back, bruised lips stretched in a grin. He asked: "What was that you was going to show me, Kelton?" It was then that Lew Dosso's gun barrel *cracked* against Rawlins's head and he spilled forward into the litter of the barnyard.

II

Ed Rawlins was still lying beside the mower when Trudy Gilder rode into the barnyard and found him. She was cradling his head on her lap when he came to. He stared into her face, shut his

15

eyes, and, when he opened them again, she was still there. He murmured: "No harps. I always thought there was harp music in heaven."

"I'm no angel," Trudy said softly, "but I thought for a minute you were. What happened?"

He told her as his fogged memory cleared. Then he said: "You said once you hated men who settled trouble with guns."

She made no answer, and, when he looked at her, there was a small smile in the corner of her lips. She was a pretty girl, this Trudy Gilder, with the darkest brown eyes Rawlins had ever seen, and hair as black as a crow's wing. Rawlins had seen pretty girls before, but he had never seen one like Trudy. He had often wondered what there was about her that set her apart from other women, and he had never been sure. He had always noted the great pride that she possessed, a sort of hewing-to-the-line quality that was in her, and now, looking up at her face, he wondered if that was it.

Rawlins sat up rubbing his aching head, and then got to his feet. He reeled uncertainly for a moment, his head whirling, and grabbed at the mower seat to steady himself. He said: "I guess you're the kind of a person who never goes back on what she says, and it wouldn't be fair of me to go ahead letting you think I'm something I'm not. You're bound to hear it sometime anyhow."

"Don't tell me, Ed." She was on her feet now,

facing him and there was a softness about her he had never seen before. "We're having a settlers' meeting tonight. Dad says it's important. That's what I came to tell you and I'm not interested in what you were. I'm only interested in what you are."

She kissed him then, a quick kiss that left a feeling of uncertainty in Rawlins and, turning from him, swiftly mounted and galloped away, a slim, lithe figure who rode gracefully and well. Rawlins didn't stir until she had disappeared into the junipers. Then he walked to the house, still a little dizzy, and sitting down on his front steps stared at the long skyline of the Cascades.

A week ago or even this morning, Rawlins would not have wished for his guns as he had when Kelton and Dosso rode up. He did not understand it. He had thought that life was entirely behind him, and Trudy had promised to marry him in the fall.

"One good crop," he had told her, "and we can build another room."

Now everything was different. Bal Tilse had done that to him; the contempt in the man's eyes was a stinging nettle across his brain. He got up and went into the house. He stared at the trunk that held his guns, walked around the room, and came back to the trunk. He had asked Tilse not to tell about his past, but Tilse had told. Ira Sills had sent his men out to make threats when talk became a little too strong against the irrigation company, but this was the first time they had gone beyond the making of threats.

Lifting the lid of the trunk, Rawlins took out the gun belts. He buckled them around him, and the weight of them on his hips was good. He lifted each gun from holster, practiced the draw, and finally slid them back into their casings, smiling in satisfaction. Gun magic, once learned as Ed Rawlins had learned it, was not easily forgotten.

Reluctantly Rawlins unbuckled the gun belts and put them back into the trunk. They weren't the way. Not yet. He fed his chickens and pigs, milked his cow, cooked supper, and shaved. He didn't know what the settlers' meeting was about, and he didn't know what Ira Sills had in mind, but he knew one thing. He wanted to lay his hands on Bal Tilse. He saddled his horse, anger slowly rising in him until it had reached the boiling point by the time he rode into Sills City.

The sun lay just above the Cascades when Rawlins tied his horse in front of the Jubilee Bar. He shouldered through the batwings, thinking that the saloon was the most likely place to find Tilse and seeing in one quick glance that he'd been right. Bal Tilse stood halfway along the bar talking to Ira Sills, and, except for the barkeep, they were the only men in the saloon. Rawlins came quickly along the bar, laid a hand on Tilse's shoulder, and brought him around, hard.

"It's a hell of a thing," Rawlins said, anger honing a sharpness to his voice, "when you see an old friend for the first time in six years and that friend rushes off as fast as his legs can carry him to blat all he knows."

"Hell, Ed," Tilse said defensively, "I told you there was nothing to be ashamed of."

"No, I'm not ashamed of anything I did then, Bal, and I'm not ashamed of what I'm doing now. But maybe you're ashamed of your double-jointed tongue that got me a beating."

"What are you talking about?" Tilse demanded.

Rawlins told him, and added: "Sills, I'd like to know what you had in mind when you sent that pair of quick-triggering saddle bums to my place."

Ira Sills was small and shrewd and smooth. He had a way of making people trust him, and he had somehow been able to duck trouble the summer before when there hadn't been a farmer on the creek whose crops had had enough water. He studied Rawlins a moment before he answered, his dark eyes hooded. Then, with unexpected frankness, he answered: "When a gunman moves into this project, I feel better when I know he's on my side. I don't want trouble, Rawlins, and I'm hoping the sample the boys showed you this afternoon will encourage you to move . . . or at least to watch your step."

"You don't know me very well, Sills."

The promoter shrugged. "There are other ways of handling a difficult situation, Rawlins. It strikes me that a man with your background would not be here posing as a farmer unless there was something in the wind."

"You wouldn't understand a man wanting to settle down, would you, Sills?"

"No, not your kind of a man," Ira Sills said.

Rawlins swung back to face Tilse. "Now you can talk, Bal, and you'd better make it good. Why did you run off at the mouth about me?"

"Don't start talking tough to me," Tilse said with sudden anger.

"I am talking tough, mister . . . and I'm still waiting to hear why you gabbed to Sills."

"When I hire out to a man," Tilse snarled, "I give him more than my gun. I thought Sills ought to know who you were, and I'm like him. I smell something that ain't in the open, and before we're done I'm gonna find out what it is."

Of all the men Rawlins had known, he had once liked Bal Tilse best. Now, looking at the gunman, he saw that there was nothing of the old feeling left. What had been a fine and strong friendship lay between them as shriveled and useless as a brown autumn leaf. Tilse was as much his enemy, now, as Lew Dosso or Jack Kelton.

"You think that a man like Sills deserves your loyalty more than a man who once fought beside you?"

"Hell, yes," Tilse snapped. "I like a man to be open and above board. You're not. I said I would find out what kind of sneaking game you're up to, and, by God . . ."

Rawlins hit him then, a short, powerful blow that caught Tilse on the side of the face and knocked him flat on his back. Tilse lay there a moment, eyes staring up at Rawlins as if not understanding this.

"A man doesn't have to take that," Sills said.

Slowly Tilse's hand came up to his cheek and touched the spot where Rawlins's fist had hit him. Then, his face scarlet, he raised himself up on his left elbow, his right hand yanking his gun.

"You've gone down a long ways, Bal," Rawlins said, "when you'll draw on a man who isn't packing a gun."

The gun was leveled in Tilse's hand. It stayed that way for a long moment, Tilse's lips twitching with the struggle that was going on in him.

Sills, moving cautiously out of the line of fire, said: "Go ahead and drill him, Tilse. Be no witnesses but me and the barkeep, and we'll tell the right story for you."

Slowly Tilse came to his feet, the gun still in his hand, the decision not yet made.

Rawlins laughed softly. "You're a better man than you think you are, Bal. You're so good that you won't be working long for a man of Sills's caliber."

It was then that Sills's office man parted the batwings, and called: "They're out here, boss!"

"All right." Sills moved away, thrusting a raucous glance at Rawlins. "I've got a lot at stake in this thing, Rawlins, and I won't let it go up in smoke. I'm hoping you won't be a damned fool and throw your life away on a fight you don't have to make."

Excitement stabbed through Ed Rawlins. The grin that broke across his bronzed, bony face held a cold challenge. "I haven't been in a fight for a long time, Sills, but I'm in this one . . . right up to my ears."

"If you aim to fight, you better start packing those guns you're supposed to be so good with," Sills retorted. "And you'd better be damned sure you have them before you meet up with Tilse again." With that, Sills motioned curtly to Tilse, and left the saloon.

A heavy sigh came out of the barkeep as the batwings flapped shut behind Sills and Tilse. He said: "Ed, I know Ira Sills pretty well. I know how far he will go . . . and, in case you don't know it, you're in trouble."

"What do you mean?"

The barkeep began mopping the mahogany, his lips compressed. He said: "I own this saloon, Ed, and it's a town where I'd like to spend the rest of my life. I think the future of this country depends on farmers who are making a good living here, and not on a bunch of them a promoter like Sills brings in because he's got a lot of land he wants settled. That's all I'm gonna say, except for one thing. Watch your back."

III

When Rawlins left the saloon, he saw the hack with a load of men in it pulling away from in front of the hotel and taking the road that led to the lower creek country. His farm was there, and so was Walt Gilder's, and half a dozen others that were the best-kept and most prosperous farms along the Purgatory.

Bal Tilse was driving the hack and Ira Sills was in the back seat. The other men in it were strangers who had probably just come in from Cassburg. Rawlins stood thoughtfully loading his pipe, and watched the hack until it disappeared. The sun was halfway down behind the Cascades now, and there was little of the day left by which these strangers could see the country, but Ira Sills, good talker that he was, didn't need much daylight to show these men what he wanted them to see along the Purgatory, and get them signed up for eighty acres of land apiece.

Rawlins crossed the street and went into the hotel. He sat down, feet cocked up on a chair in front of him, and, pulling steadily at his pipe, gave thought to this thing as he saw it now. He had shirked his responsibility, and shame was in him because of it. He had not gone to any of the settlers' meetings; he had paid little attention to Ira Sills's moves, and, except for exchanging a little work with Walt Gilder and courting Trudy, he had lived within himself almost entirely.

It had been wrong, all wrong, and he saw it now as he had not seen it before. He had the choice of running, which was what Sills wanted him to do, or of staying and conducting a one-man fight against Sills. His chances of winning that fight were close to zero. He had been through too many not to take cognizance of the odds. He needed help but whether the farmers would listen to him and whether they'd fight if they did listen was something he seriously doubted.

Rawlins was still in the hotel lobby when darkness came, and lights bloomed along the street. The hack stopped in front of the hotel, and the strangers got down, talked for a long time with Sills, and then came in while the hack wheeled away. Rawlins stepped in front of them and asked: "Are you men thinking of taking land here?"

They were farmers, blunt-fingered men with faces weathered by wind and sun. They were much like other settlers who lived along the Purgatory, big-muscled men who felt a little cramped in their store clothes.

"That's right," one of them answered. "We're from Wagontown, on the other side of the hump.

We figgered it was time we quit renting and started in owning our land."

"Has anybody told you we didn't get the water we needed last year?" Rawlins asked.

The men exchanged quick glances and nodded, as if expecting this. The spokesman said: "I don't know why men who live here now would try to discourage further settlement, but I'm telling you something, mister. All the big talk you put out won't stop us. More than that, it won't stop a thousand others from crossing the mountains to live here. We like the looks of this country, and we're staying."

They started around him as if satisfied that he'd been told enough, but Rawlins wasn't finished. He stepped in front of them again and said: "You owe it to yourselves to come to the settlers' meeting tonight."

"It would be a waste of time," one of the men said sullenly. "We were told by Mister Sills that there is a group of settlers here who want to hog this whole segregation, and are doing all they can to buck him and discourage others who want to come. Well, we'll have no part of it. Now if you'll step aside, we'll go to our rooms."

Rawlins watched them go up the stairs and muttered: "Fools! Damned, stubborn fools."

"With their life savings in their pockets and bent on spending it," a man behind Rawlins said. As Rawlins turned, the man held out his hand. "The name's McCann. Sam McCann from Portland."

"Ed Rawlins," Rawlins said as he shook hands. "I guess I've got a talent for sticking my nose into other men's business. Only thing is the more of those yahoos who come in, the less water there is for the rest of us."

McCann was a tall, lantern-jawed man with corn-colored hair that successfully pointed in several directions. He had a pencil thrust behind one ear; several sheets of paper were stuffed into a coat pocket, and his general appearance was that of an animated scarecrow. He studied Rawlins for a moment. Finally he said: "I've heard of you. You're the farmer who's had quite a past as a gunslinger, aren't you?"

"That's right," Rawlins answered. "That story seems to have traveled."

"Sounds like a good story," McCann said. "I'm a reporter, Rawlins, and I've always got my ears open for something that's good. It strikes me this is good."

"There's nothing about my life that would make a good story," Rawlins murmured, and, moving toward the door, he went through it and turned toward the schoolhouse.

"All right," McCann said, catching up with Rawlins, "we'll let your life story go, but I think you'll help me do the job I'm down here for. You know, of course, that these irrigation projects around Cassburg make up a huge amount of acreage and will furnish homes for thousands of people if properly operated."

"Which this one isn't," Rawlins snapped.

"I was wondering," McCann persisted, "about that very thing. Now around Cassburg everything seems to be in order, but it's Ira Sills who does most of the advertising, and I expect a thousand families to move in here before fall."

"Look, McCann." Rawlins paused, and faced the reporter. "How can a thousand families make a living here when we didn't get enough water last summer?"

"Perhaps they won't, but they're like these men you just talked to. They have some money saved, and they want to own their land. That money will go into Ira Sills's hands, and their starving is not a problem that will worry Mister Sills."

"I guess you've about got it," Rawlins agreed sourly. He told McCann about Kelton and Dosso visiting him that afternoon, and added: "I guess that was Sills's way of trying to get me out of the country."

"Rawlins, it looks like the beginning of a story here. If I had a good one, I'd splash it across the front page of my paper, and it would be read all over the Northwest. That's the only way I know to stop these people from believing Sills's advertising."

"You want a good story, do you, McCann?"

Rawlins said softly. "All right, I'll give you one, but you may not live long enough to print it. Come along. We'll go see what this settlers' meeting is all about."

The schoolhouse was jammed. Rawlins, pushing his way through the crowd that stood just inside the door, saw that most of the fifty settlers living along Purgatory Creek were here. They were a somber-faced lot, the women and children filling the seats, the men standing around the back of the room and along the sides.

Walt Gilder, president of the Purgatory Creek Settlers' Association, pounded on the desk in front of the room, and Rawlins, jostled to one side by the late-comers, saw Lew Dosso and Jack Kelton on one side of him, and Bal Tilse on the other. Sills's office man was there, but Sills was not. Gilder told the secretary to read the minutes of the last meeting, and, after he'd sat down, Gilder asked if there was any new business to be brought up. The crowd shifted, shuffling feet, and the ripple of talk made a restlessness in the room. Gilder pounded for order, and tried to glower, but a successful glower was not in Walt Gilder. He was a little, red-cheeked man who looked more like Santa Claus than he did a farmer, but the spirit of resistance was in him, and it was Rawlins's feeling that Gilder was one of the few in the room who could be counted on if it came to a finish fight.

"Well," Gilder said, "this here meeting was called for a definite purpose, and the sooner we get to discussing it, the better. We 'bout starved last summer, and things don't look too good this year. A sinkhole showed up on the other side of the butte so the settlers on the lateral didn't get water for a week. The company was too busy to fix it, so some of us took a day off and did it ourselves. Seeing as this project is supposed to be supervised by the state, it appears to me that it's time for us to make a kick to the right people. Now I'd like to hear some discussion."

Again there was that shifting of bodies and scraping of feet, but no one wanted to talk. Rawlins looked at the crowd, saw there would be no determined resistance from them.

"Most of you come quite a piece to get here," Gilder said testily. "You gonna sit here like a bunch of wooden heads just 'cause you're scared of Ira Sills's toughs?"

A man jumped up. "We shouldn't talk that way in meeting, Walt. Mebbe we just better wait through the summer, and see what kind of service we'll get."

"The ditches aren't any bigger than they were last summer," Gilder snapped, "and they didn't carry enough water then."

Jack Kelton grinned broadly and nudged Lew Dosso. On the other side of the room, Bal Tilse watched Rawlins. Sam McCann growled an oath

29

in Rawlins's ear, and said: "They're scared to open their mouths."

"All right," Gilder said in disgust, "might as well adjourn the meeting. But at least go home and think about it. Mebbe you figger you can hang on till hell freezes over, but I can't. I've got to have a crop if me and my girl are gonna eat."

"Walt," Rawlins said, and stepped forward, "I've got something to say."

Walt Gilder grinned. "Go ahead," he said. "You sure got the floor in this meeting."

The women and children turned to see who it was, and for the first time Rawlins saw that Trudy was there. Indecision halted him for a minute. Trudy wouldn't like what he was going to say. Then he gritted his teeth, put his hands on the back of the seat in front of him, and began to talk.

"The way I see this thing," he began, "it isn't so much a proposition of enlarging the ditches and telling the state about what's going on as it is informing the people who might be settlers here that there just isn't enough water in Purgatory Creek to go around. There's four men at the hotel who were taken out to see some farms by Ira Sills this afternoon. Now they want to settle here. What's more, they got sore because I told them we didn't get the water we were supposed to last summer. They said there'd be a thousand others crossing the mountains to settle here. I'm asking you men just where would we or Ira Sills or anybody else find water to irrigate the thirty thousand acres that Sills has in this segregation?"

"There never was that much water in Purgatory Creek." Gilder nodded.

"Sills knows that," Rawlins went on. "A while ago somebody said we shouldn't talk about Sills's toughs. Now maybe we ought to be scared out of our shirts. I ought to be, because they came out to my place and beat me up today. I'm scared, all right, but I'm gonna make my holler just the same. I'm gonna holler so loud that these suckers coming in are going to find out this valley isn't just what Ira Sills tells 'em it is."

The issue that faced the settlers had never been put into words the way Ed Rawlins had just put it, and Ira Sills's name had never been publicly mentioned before. It seemed to all the settlers except Walt Gilder that it was something like treason to talk this way, and for a long moment there was only silence, tight, tense, and filled with a grim foreboding.

Jack Kelton wasn't grinning now. He made a step toward Rawlins, but Lew Dosso whispered something in his ear, and the two of them pushed their way through the crowd and left the school-house. Bal Tilse still watched Rawlins, his lean face puzzled and uncertain.

"Anybody else got something to say?" Gilder demanded. "When you got a man with Ed Rawlins's spunk in the crowd, there oughta be somebody else who's got guts enough to back him."

"I don't call it spunk!" a man shouted. "He's a gunfighter . . . a killer. We all got that word today, and I'm thinking he's here for some purpose that ain't good. I never seen him at a settlers' meeting before."

"Neither did I!" another called out.

"Gunfighters thrive on trouble!" a third man yelled. "Might be his way of getting a job. We've got wives and kids, but Ed Rawlins ain't."

"You're a bunch of old women!" Walt Gilder roared. "Damn' yellow-backed old women who are scared of your shadow! I'm resigning this here job you gave me. I think I'm a man, and I know danged well I don't want no office in an outfit that . . ."

A gun blazed outside, the slug slapping through a window. Again it roared. The two wall lamps winked out. A flame leaped ceilingward, caught a curtain, and seemed to explode.

Fire! The cry came out of the men, shrill and scared, and panic was upon them as they broke for the door. Some thought of their families, some only of themselves. Rawlins knocked a man down with his fist who plunged for the door. At the same instant he shouted: "Keep that door clear, you fools! Let the women and children out first."

But Ed Rawlins might as well have tried to stop a stampede.

IV

Men had jammed into the doorway, wedged tightly, and now could not move. Bal Tilse, cursing and swinging his gun barrel, battered men out of the way and somehow cleared the doorway. Rawlins, McCann, and Gilder got to the windows on the side away from the fire, kicked glass from the frames, and helped the children and the women through. Within a matter of minutes the schoolhouse was empty, and barely in time. Rawlins stood in the fringe of light, an arm around Trudy, and watched the walls cave in, a great column of sparks and flames rising skyward.

"Awful lucky," Sam McCann muttered.

"Won't be no school for our kids this winter," a man said.

"We'll build another one!" Walt Gilder shouted.

"You donate the labor, and I'll put up the money." It was Ira Sills standing there, not ten feet from Ed Rawlins. "Education for our children is the most important thing we have. Whatever happens, we must not let it go."

A smart move, Rawlins thought, the sort of move that could be expected from Sills and one that would make it doubly hard to get any co-operation from the settlers. Whether Dosso and Kelton had fired the shots upon Sills's orders, or whether it had been their own notion, was something Rawlins would never know, but he had a hunch that the idea was to plunge the schoolhouse into darkness and produce a panic for the purpose of stopping the discussion Gilder and Rawlins had started. Probably the fire was a result they had not foreseen, but, in any case, Sills had cleverly turned it to his advantage.

"If your gunslingers hadn't started the fire, Sills," Rawlins said, "you wouldn't have to put up the money."

"Can you prove who fired those shots?" Sills demanded.

"No, but Dosso and Kelton left the schoolhouse just before the shots were fired."

Sills laughed scornfully. "That proves nothing! As a matter of fact, they came over to my office to report about this sinkhole we failed to fix. I'm sorry about that, but we were busy at the time. We'll see it doesn't happen again, even if we have to double our maintenance crew."

"You'd better keep your mouth shut, Rawlins!" a man cried. "We've got kids to go to school, and you ain't. I think that's a fine offer Mister Sills has just made."

Rawlins said softly: "Come along, McCann. You, too, Walt."

Holding Trudy's arm, he beat a path for her through the crowd toward the hotel. Always before Rawlins had fought for pay, and the men who had hired him and those who fought beside him had given him complete co-operation. He was not fighting for pay now; it was a common fight where all the interests were the same, and yet there was no co-operation at all. There was even resentment among the settlers because he wanted to fight.

"You can't get those men to fight, Rawlins," McCann said. "They don't understand."

"The damned fools!" Gilder said heatedly.

They were in front of the hotel, the light from the window falling across Trudy's face, and pride came into Ed Rawlins then. He was proud of this girl who had promised to marry him, proud of their dreams.

He asked: "Are you mad, Trudy?"

"No," she answered quickly, "but what are you going to do now?"

"What I do depends on McCann." He motioned to the reporter. "He said he would spread our story all over the front page of his paper, if it was a good one. What about it, McCann?"

"It's a good one, Rawlins." The reporter grinned. "A damned good one, and that fire was what made it extra good. I'm hiring a rig to take me to Cassburg in the morning so I can catch the stage to Shaniko." He pulled the pencil down from his ear and reached for the paper in his pocket. "Right now I want a few facts about the total acreage in the segregation, the size of the present farms, the amount of water in the Purgatory, and so on."

"Walt can give that to you," Rawlins said. "Trudy, let's go home. Where's your horse?"

"In front of the Mercantile."

"I'm glad to have met you, Rawlins." McCann shook Rawlins's hand. "It's a funny thing in this state. On the other side of the Cascades life goes on just about as it has for generations. Over here it's new and tough and damned near primitive. That's why these folks who come from there are a little slow seeing that they have to do their own fighting. Give them time, Rawlins. Meanwhile, I'll give you a story that'll put a crimp in Mister Sills's plans."

"Thanks, McCann," Rawlins said, and crossed the street to his horse.

There was little talk between Rawlins and Trudy on the way home, but, after her horse had been put away, they faced each other in front of her house, her face a pale oval in the darkness.

Rawlins said: "I wanted to tell you this afternoon what I'd been, but now you know. Does it make any difference?"

"I told you then it's what you are now that counts, Ed," the girl said softly, "not what you were when you rode with Bal Tilse. I'm proud of you and what you did tonight."

"It may not be over," Rawlins said somberly. "Sills is afraid of me or he wouldn't have sent Kelton and Dosso after me. After what I said tonight, he'll have to get me. I know about men

36

like him, Trudy. I know how they work. They have to keep going, have to keep folks iced into line, or they're done."

She was silent a moment as if thinking about it, and then she said: "I guess I've felt the way I do because of Dad. We've been through these things before, and he always fights just like he's fighting now. He'll get killed, Ed. And if you die, too, then there'll be nothing left. I lost a brother three years ago. He was shot in the back and left in the sagebrush to die. It was like this. I can't stand to go through it again."

"But is there any sense in losing the things you've dreamed about and worked for just because you won't fight for them?" he asked roughly.

"Forty years ago people out here had to do these things. It was fight or die. That was the life people lived, and they knew it and understood it. It's different now. If I'm going to have your children, Ed, I want them growing up in a world that can give them security."

"They'll never have security on the Purgatory if we don't fight for it now," he said stubbornly.

She started to say something, and whirled away instead and ran into the house. Rawlins waited until he heard the door slam, and then mounted and rode away, the feeling in him that a man has when he sees his life's treasure slipping out of his hand and is powerless to hold it.

Rawlins made his bed outside that night, his guns loaded and beside him on the ground. Sills's next move would be fast and ruthless, and there was no sense in dying in his shack like a trapped rat. The settlers would not fight now, but they would if driven far enough, and another crop failure might touch off the dynamite.

It was dawn when Rawlins awoke, and the thought that had been in his mind when he went to sleep was still there, and with it was another thought. Sills would kill Walt Gilder. Rawlins swore he had been so sure Sills would strike at him first that he had forgotten Walt completely. He latched his belts around him, saddled his horse, and started back toward Gilder's place, cursing himself for not having foreseen Sills's move sooner. Rawlins did not hold the settlers' trust; Walt Gilder did, and for that reason Gilder was more dangerous in the long run to Ira Sills's plans.

The light was still thin when Rawlins, topping a ridge north of his farm, saw the vague form of a rider, then heard the muffled *thud* of fast-traveling hoofs in the sandy soil. Rawlins reined off the road and pulled a gun, despair, then cold fury rising in him. He had been too late! That was his first thought. The rider had killed Walt Gilder, and was coming on after him.

Rawlins waited a full five minutes until the rider was within fifty feet of him. Then he reined into the road, his gun cocked, and called: "Pull up!"

It was Bal Tilse who yanked his horse to a stop. He said—"Easy on that trigger, Ed."—and made no move for his gun.

"What are you doing here?" Rawlins asked.

Tilse laid a steady gaze on Rawlins's face. "I'm a fool, Ed, the damnedest, most muddle-headed fool that ever walked this earth! I figured when I heard you were here that you were holding down some gunslinging job, and I had an idea to get you to throw in with me and we'd do a little bounty chasing. Then I got here, and found out you weren't even packing a gun, you were just a farmer, and I got sore. I guess I wasn't so sore at you as I was at myself. You were doing the thing I'd always wanted to, Ed, and I'm so damned small I pretended to think you'd gone plumb to the bottom."

Bal Tilse wasn't lying. Rawlins saw that, and he asked softly: "What set you straight?"

"It's like you said in the Jubilee. I'm too good a man to be working for a skunk like Sills. I lost my head after you walloped me, and pulled my gun. Sills wanted me to smoke you down. I guess that started it. Then that business of burning the schoolhouse. A lot of people might have got burned to death, and what Sills is after isn't worth it. Sills was up all night thinking what he was gonna do. He got me and Dosso and Kelton up about an hour ago and gave us our orders. I was supposed to come out here and bushwhack Walt Gilder, then get you. Ed, I've done some killing, but, by hell, I never bushwhacked a man in my life, and Ira Sills doesn't have enough money to get me to."

"What about Dosso and Kelton?"

"Dosso heard what you and Gilder and McCann said in front of the hotel. He'd told Sills, and Sills says the one thing that can beat him is for a big daily like McCann's paper to run that story. Kelton is to drive the rig with McCann aboard this morning, and he'll have a team that isn't broke. About the same time they get to the top of the grade on the other side of the Purgatory, Dosso will cut loose with a few shots, and scare the team. Kelton makes a jump, and the rig will go over the grade with McCann inside."

"When are they pulling out?"

"They're probably gone by now."

"Bal, how are you playing this game from here on in?"

"Son, I'm right behind you! And when this is all buttoned up, if you want a partner who doesn't know nothing but trigger pulling, I'm with you."

"You're signed up, Bal." Rawlins held out his hand, and Tilse shook it. "If we ride straight for the creek, we'll probably beat Kelton's rig to the foot of the grade. Chances are Dosso is forted up behind a lava pile that's just north of where the road comes over the rim. If you can get McCann out of that buggy, I'll handle Dosso."

"I'll do it," Tilse promised.

They stayed together until they reached the creek, and Rawlins said: "You better hit for the road, Bal. Good luck."

Tilse grinned, and swung upstream. Rawlins rode as nearly straight up the east wall of the cañon as he could, angling among boulders, and gradually working downstream to where an ancient tributary had worn a passage through the rimrock that lifted a sheer thirty feet above Rawlins.

It brought Rawlins to the plateau above the Purgatory about two miles downstream from where Lew Dosso would be holed up, a long way around but the only way because, if he had tried to come up the road, he'd have been shot out of his saddle by Dosso before he reached the plateau, and there was no other break through the sheer cliffs on the east side of the Purgatory for ten miles.

Rawlins paused to blow his horse, and saw the buggy cross the creek and start up the grade. Bal Tilse was not in sight, and for a moment Rawlins felt doubt break across his mind. Ira Sills might have set up a bushwhack trap, using Bal Tilse to lure Rawlins into it. Then he put that from his mind. He had gone too far now to doubt Tilse.

Making a swing into the junipers away from the

rim, Rawlins came presently to the road and turned toward the Purgatory, his gun palmed. It was then that gunfire blasted apart the morning quiet, and Rawlins thought he was too late. He saw Dosso the same instant the gunman saw him, and they fired together. He made a high target in the saddle, and there was only Dosso's head and shoulders above the lava, but Dosso, surprised by Rawlins's sudden appearance and the firing from the cañon, missed his first shot and paid the penalty for having missed. His second shot was nothing more than a finger twitching in death, the slug burying itself in the dirt below him. Rawlins's bullet had caught him between the eyes.

There was no more firing from the road below Rawlins, but he heard the run of horses, and he put spurs to his own mount. He came around the first bend in the grade, saw the approaching team running hard, Kelton hanging onto the lines and weaving drunkenly in the seat. Rawlins reined his mount toward the bank, and then a cry came from him, for the team swung too near the edge, loose dirt giving way under them, and then plunged off into space, Kelton's scream riding above the roar of landsliding rocks and dirt.

Bal Tilse came into sight, his cocked gun in his hand, saw Rawlins looking over the edge, and called: "What happened?"

"Dosso's dead, and Kelton just went off. It isn't a pretty sight, Bal. A hell of a way to die, even for Jack Kelton."

"He had one of my slugs in him," Tilse said. "I beat 'em to the foot of the grade, came part way up, and pulled in behind a pile of rocks. When they got close, I rode out and covered Kelton, telling McCann to jump. McCann jumped, but Kelton allowed he'd smoke it out with me. I reckon he was shot so bad he couldn't hang onto his team."

McCann was waiting for them in the road, puzzled and angry, and, when he saw Rawlins, he shouted: "Life over here isn't primitive, Rawlins! It's just plain savage. By the time I get done writing my story, there won't be anybody but tough hands who'd want to live over here."

"You still figure you've got a good story?" Rawlins asked.

A grin spread across McCann's dusty face. "Mister, I had enough of a story last night, but it gets better all the time. Fact is, I don't think I'd live long if it got any better than it is now."

"You're lucky you're alive this long," Rawlins said dryly. "You ride my horse, McCann, or you won't get to Cassburg in time to catch the stage. Bal, you'd better ride with him. Tell the deputy in Cassburg what happened."

"I'm not stopping in Cassburg, Ed," Tilse said. "I'm going to Portland with this gent, and I'm not coming back until I've got a copy of the paper with this story in headlines a foot high."

"You'll get them," McCann promised.

It was late that afternoon when Rawlins stopped at the Gilder farm. Trudy was making a strawberry pie, and there was a patch of flour across her forehead that made Rawlins grin and hand her a towel and remark on her "dirty face."

"Stay for supper," Trudy said, "and, while you're waiting, tell me what happened."

"You're sure something's happened?"

"It's written all over you," she said. "Go on."

He told her, then, and added: "I had a little talk with Sills when I came through town. I never saw him scared before but, when he found out that Dosso and Kelton were dead, he was plenty scared. Then I topped that off by telling him that Tilse will repeat what he planned for me and your dad, and Sills started begging. He may go to jail before it's over, but he's sure going to sell out here."

"If Tilse hadn't been the man he was," Trudy mused, "you and Dad would have been murdered."

"That's right, but, after I hit Bal yesterday, Sills figured he'd enjoy beefing me. It goes to prove that there's different levels of honor in all occupations, which same is true with gunfighting like everything else. I knew about Tilse, but I wasn't sure when he'd find it out." He came to her then, and took her hand in his. Her eyes went down to his guns, and, when they lifted to his face, he asked: "What's the answer, Trudy?"

"You're right," she said simply. "I didn't see it until you said last night that if our children were to have security here, we had to fight for it . . . now. I'm proud of you, Ed."

He kissed her then. "Maybe we'd better not wait for that room." He grinned.

She smiled. "I'll be ready, Ed . . . tomorrow."

IT'S HELL TO BE A HERO!

I

Nobody in the town of San Rafael considered Ed Casey a hero, not even Ed Casey himself. He was an ordinary man, a lawyer in his late twenties, sandy-haired and blue-eyed, and possessed of a good pair of shoulders. Single, he was mild-mannered, and respected for his integrity.

Then the Potter gang knocked over Eli Scoggins's bank, and Casey's way of life was forever changed.

It started the day before hunting season opened. Casey left his office shortly after 12:00 p.m. and stepped into Abbot's Hardware to get the .30-30 he had left to be worked on. He bought a package of shells and loaded the rifle, thinking he'd walk across the creek and take a few shots to see if the sights were true.

Lou Abbot joshed him a little about how many bucks he expected to get. Casey was the best shot in San Rafael, and, when he went out with a party of townsmen, he usually got as many as the others added together. Casey said he'd be satisfied with six, paid Abbot, and left the store.

Just as Casey stepped on the boardwalk, two men ran out of the bank, one carrying a heavily weighted gunny sack. A third man held their horses in the street. The instant they hit saddles, Fred Bent, Scoggins's teller, let out a squall that the bank had been robbed. One of the outlaws put a bullet through the window and Bent let out another squall that had a different tone.

Casey acted purely on instinct. He let go with his first shot before the outlaws had traveled ten feet, knocking the lead man out of his saddle. There was a lot of dust then, the other two cracking steel to their mounts at every jump. Casey missed his second shot because of the dust, but he tallied number two with his third bullet. The remaining outlaw, the one with the gunny sack, made the corner and was out of sight.

Casey wheeled into the store and charged along the counter, slamming into Lou Abbot and piling him up on a keg of nails. Abbot yelped and came upright. Casey raced through the back door to the alley. The third bank robber was departing for open country when Casey let go with another shot. The man threw up his hands and plunged out of the saddle, the gunny sack disappearing into the sagebrush.

There was plenty of excitement after that. Everybody was in the street yelling questions and answers that were less than half-truths. Doc Miller took a look at Fred Bent and said: "Get him over to my office. He's hit pretty hard."

Eli Scoggins, the bank owner, sat on the floor, his narrow face lowered to his knees. He rocked back and forth, moaning. The sheriff, Pete Ennis, appeared from somewhere, and began bawling orders that achieved nothing. By the time folks caught on to what had happened, Casey was back with the gunny sack.

"Here you are, Eli." Casey dropped the sack beside the banker. "You didn't lose a nickel."

Scoggins and Casey had had one thing in common for years—their low opinion of each other. Now Scoggins sat there and blinked at Casey as if he didn't see him at all. *Shock,* Casey thought. It was the first time he had ever seen the banker unable to talk.

There was a lot of handshaking and back-slapping, and a deal of talk about Casey being a hero and how much the town owed him. The sheriff came in and announced that all three Potters were dead, and it was a good thing on account of it saved the state hanging money.

"There was a big reward out for them murdering *hombres,*" Ennis said. "Five thousand, I think. You'll get it all, Ed."

Casey blinked. $5,000! He'd never seen that much money in his life. Then Lou Abbot yelled: "I guess Eli will add something to it, Ed!"

Scoggins came awake in a hurry. He grabbed the gunny sack and jumped up. "The hell I will. Casey gets the reward. That's good wages for one day."

"Damned skinflint," Abbot growled to himself.

Casey saw Lola Horn then and he got through the crowd to her. Lola was the town teacher and the only reason Casey was glad he was chairman of the school board.

Now she laid a hand on his arm. "It was wonderful, Ed. Looks as if you've been unappreciated around here."

He grinned. "I know one place where I've been unappreciated."

It was Casey's opinion she was the prettiest woman in San Rafael.

She smiled. "Perhaps you could change that, Ed."

They walked along the street toward the schoolhouse. Lola was lovely, Casey thought again as he gazed at her, with her cricket-black hair and dark eyes, and a disconcerting way of keeping her distance from single men in town.

Now there was no trace of the chill manner. Casey walked in silence, wondering about it. Lola's hand was still on his arm, and she held her head proudly as if she wanted everyone to notice whom she was with.

For weeks Casey had been trying to work up enough nerve to propose, but he'd been afraid to risk it. Now he had a hunch she'd say yes. The time to strike was when the iron was hot, but doubts took possession of him.

Maybe she'd heard Ennis say there was a reward coming, and he sure didn't want a woman marrying him for his money—a consideration that had not been a cause of worry before.

It was nearly 1:00 p.m. when they reached the schoolhouse. The yard was filled with children, too many for one teacher. San Rafael needed a two-teacher school, but it was a reform Casey had been unable to achieve because of Scoggins's opposition. An idea took root in his mind as he paused outside the door. Scoggins owed him now.

"Come inside," Lola said.

She closed the door behind them. She put both hands on his arms and looked up at him. "Ed, I know I haven't been here long, but I think I know these people. They have very short memories."

He didn't know what she meant, and this was not the time to go into it. Her lips came together. He leaned down and kissed her. It seemed like the thing to do, something he'd wanted to do for a long time except that he'd never had the nerve.

He wasn't disappointed. It was a nice kiss with her arms around his neck, a kiss that set his heart to pounding.

"I'll see you tonight?" he asked.

"Of course, Ed."

As he walked back to town, he wondered why she'd let him kiss her. He had figured she'd slap his ears off if he tried it. Then came a suspicion he didn't like. Maybe it was because he'd become a hero. Some women were like that, he'd heard. He couldn't believe Lola was, but she had definitely changed her attitude toward him.

Still, he thought glumly, he loved her and figured he'd better speak his piece while she was in the mood.

Casey stopped at Doc Miller's office and learned Fred Bent would live, but he'd be on his back for a long time. Bent was the one good thing about the bank. It would be like Scroggins to fire him when he didn't come to work in the morning.

Casey crossed the street to the bank. Scroggins had been a millstone around San Rafael's neck for years and no one seemed willing to do anything about it. He was cool and scheming, and had a talent for keeping his political fences mended. There was no doubt the sheriff was his man—a very handy situation when Scroggins stepped outside the law to beat down a business competitor.

Scroggins had been able to use his financial power to get a stranglehold on every business in the county except the Yankee Boy Mine. The one person who had successfully defied him was Julia Anderson, the mine owner.

Now that Casey thought about Julia, an idea lingering in his mind flowered.

There was no one in the bank when Casey went in except Scroggins himself, in the vault putting the money away. Casey went through the gate at the end of the rail and stood watching Scroggins fondling the coins as if they were the most precious things on earth.

"I want to talk to you, Scroggins."

Surprised, he whirled around, dropping a handful of gold eagles on the floor. They *jingled* musically and rolled away in a half dozen directions.

"What do you mean, sneaking up on me like that?"

"I want to talk to you."

No one used that tone of voice on Eli Scoggins. Not even Julia Larson. He stepped out of the vault, scowling. "I'm not paying you a reward, Casey."

"I don't expect any."

"I'm not throwing any business your way, either. When I need a lawyer, I'll use a man who's dry behind the ears."

Anger rose in Casey. "I don't want any business from you."

Scoggins sat down at his desk and leaned back in the swivel chair. "What in hell do you want?"

"Fred's got a wife and six kids."

"So?"

"What are you going to do to help him while he's laid up?"

"Nothing. He'll be back to work in a day or two."

"No, he won't. He got a slug in his chest. Doc says he'll be laid up for weeks."

"If Bent had kept his damned mouth shut, he wouldn't have gotten himself shot up."

Casey eyed him. "Maybe you wanted your bank robbed."

Scoggins jumped up and motioned to the door, his hand trembling in rage. "Damn you, Casey. Get out!"

"Not till I find out a couple things. Are you going to pay Fred's salary until he's able to come back here?"

"No."

"Another thing. The school needs an addition."

"I've told you ten times . . . I won't stand for that."

"The school will get more crowded with the Yankee Boy taking on more men. New families will be moving in."

Scoggins pounded a fist on the desk. "I'm not blind, Casey. You figure I'll bow down and scrape to you because some damned fools called you a hero. Well, you're no hero to me. You're just a shyster who happened to be handy with a Winchester when my bank was held up. I've licked you on this school business before, and I'll do again. Now, will you get out?"

"Yeah," Casey said. "There's only so much skunk smell I can stand at one time."

He walked out, feeling the pressure of the banker's eyes on him. Maybe he was acting the fool. Folks got along better in San Rafael if they didn't buck Scoggins. The banker made it tough for anyone who got in his way. That was where Casey took his hat off to Julia Larson.

Most people in San Rafael didn't like Julia.

Some even said she wasn't a good woman, maybe because she was doing a man's job in handling the Yankee Boy Mine. Or perhaps it was because she had a way with men that made other woman jealous. That was Casey's private opinion, but one no woman he knew would corroborate. In any case, she was a fighter, and Casey respected fighters.

II

Lou Abbot was in the back of the store talking to half a dozen townsmen when Casey walked in. Abbot stopped, saw who it was, and let out a whoop. "Speak of the devil!"

There was more talk about Casey's being the town's hero and saving everybody's money, and putting San Rafael on the map. Then Casey couldn't stand it any longer.

"That's enough of this palaver, boys. I'm no hero. You know it as well as I do."

"It takes sand in a man's craw . . . ," Abbot began.

"Hell," Casey broke in, "you'd have done the same thing if you had been in my boots."

"I sure wouldn't have shot as straight."

They laughed. Then Casey said: "Scoggins agrees I'm not a hero. He says I'm just a shyster who happened to be handy with a Winchester."

There was no laughter then. They looked at each

other, and then they looked at the floor. Abbot reached into the keg at his feet for a handful of nails. "You damned near punctured me when you shoved me down on these, Ed."

Still no one laughed.

Casey said: "It's Scoggins I'd like to puncture, and I've got an idea how to do it."

"*Aw,* let's forget Scoggins," Abe Rucker said. He was the newspaper editor, but as far as he was concerned Eli Scoggins's activities were beyond the reach of the press. "Go ahead and tell him, Lou."

"Well, we're damned ashamed of Scoggins," Abbot said bluntly. "Bucking civic improvements because they'll raise taxes is one thing, but the way he took what you done is something else."

"Thought we were going to forget Scoggins," Casey said.

"We can't, and Abe knows it. Anyhow, you did something that was a benefit to all of us, so we're fixing to have a feed tonight to show our appreciation. Maybe have a medal struck off."

The idea that had been working in Casey's mind now spurted into full bloom. "That's mighty thoughtful of you boys. Is Scoggins invited?"

There was an awkward moment of silence before Abbot said: "He'll be there if we have to drag him. Besides, his wife wouldn't miss a social event."

"About that medal. Wouldn't it be better if you

got up a subscription list? I don't aim to use the money for myself, but it fits into my idea for trimming Scoggins down."

They looked at each other, the kind of look a bunch of rabbits might give each other when they were considering going after the fox. There was some head scratching and ear pulling and a deal of hesitation.

"Look," Casey said, "we all feel the same way about Scoggins. It just happens that right now I'm in position to go after him. Give me some ammunition, and I'll do the job."

"All right," Rucker agreed reluctantly. "I might be able to find some room in the paper."

"One more thing," Casey said. "Is this going to be for women?"

Abbot nodded. "Sure. Lola can sit beside you."

Casey grinned. "Now, that's right generous, with Abe feeling about Lola like he does."

They laughed again, all but Rucker who looked down his long nose and muttered something about lawyers.

They were still laughing, all feeling good again until Casey said: "Let's invite Julia Larson."

He might as well have dangled a skeleton in front of them. The laughing stopped. There was some more head scratching and shifting around before Abbot said: "Damn it, Ed, have you gone clear off your nut? You know what that woman is?"

"I know she's smart enough to make money and manage a payroll," Casey said. "I've heard the gossip. Maybe she does wear her skirts too short and she tears around at crazy times of night and she runs a business without asking some man to do it, but nobody knows if any of the rest of it is true."

"You know how women feel about her," Abbot muttered.

"Then let the rest of the women stay home," Casey said.

"You can't do it, Ed."

"Ask her, Lou," Casey insisted. "I aim to beat Eli down a peg, and having the one person at the table tonight who has stopped him the way Julia has would just about fix things."

Abbot threw the handful of nails back into the keg. "All right, Ed. I don't know what you're thinking, but I'll invite her. It's a damn' fool mistake. You'll see."

Casey left his office early that afternoon, but there was no escaping the halo fate had hung on him. People stopped him on the street to shake hands. School children stood motionlessly, staring solemnly. Then he caught the buzz of talk.

"Got all three Potters."

"Shot them dead."

"Bravest man in San Rafael."

"Bet he gets Duke Dorsey next time that outlaw rides into town."

That made Casey squirm. It was a new thought, and he hoped nobody else got the notion. Duke Dorsey would kill anyone for a price. He was the fastest man with a gun in the county, and, now that Casey thought about it, he was the kind who might show up just to challenge him. That would be the end of Ed Casey. He was no hand with a revolver.

Mrs. Davis, Casey's landlady, met him at the door, beaming with pride.

"Look, Missus Davis," he said, "I've boarded here ever since I put up my shingle. Did you ever figure I was a hero?"

His words wiped the smile off her face. "Well, to be right honest, Ed, I guess none of us knew. But I think it's wonderful. We all do. Why, there's talk of making you mayor."

Casey groaned, and went up to his room. By the time he had taken a bath, shaved, and got into his best suit, it was time to go after Lola. He started out through the back, intending to go down a side street, when Mrs. Davis called: "Ed! Wait a minute, Ed. I hitched up the buggy for you. Nothing's too good for our hero."

"If you don't quit this hero stuff . . ." Casey stopped when he saw Mrs. Davis's face.

"I thought you'd like to take Lola for a ride after the shindig," she said.

Mrs. Davis owned a pair of matched bays and the newest buggy in San Rafael with the reddest wheels. Casey thanked her.

He got in and headed down Main, gritting his teeth and deciding a hero had no business taking a side street. The strange part of the whole business was that Mrs. Davis never let anyone drive her bays.

Lola was ready when Casey got to her place. She was something to make a man look twice. She wore a blue silk dress that rustled when she walked, a blue bonnet on her black hair, and she carried a blue parasol.

Casey thought about that kiss in the school-house, so he asked: "Let's take a ride. They won't start until we get there."

"I guess they won't," she said.

He took the creek road out of town, contemplating the gloom-shadowed life of a hero. Then he reached the cottonwood grove and put his mind to more pleasant things. He slid an arm around Lola. Nothing happened except that she looked up at him. He kissed her.

It was a kiss to remember. When she finally drew back, she asked: "How long have I known you, Ed?"

He fumbled around for words. "Ever since you got here. I guess we'd better get back."

The dinner came off as expected except that Julia didn't show up. Casey asked Abbot, who shrugged in silent reply. Casey had a hunch Mrs. Abbot had stopped it.

The local Circle of the Royal Women chapter of the Throne of St. George put the meal on. Scoggins was there with Mrs. Scoggins, a small, sharp-tongued woman who ruled the Scoggins home as effectively as he ruled the business life of the county.

After ice cream and cake there was a deal of speech making about Casey's heroism that kept him fidgeting and red-faced. Then some songs and some more speeches, including a touching tribute from Abe Rucker. If there had been a hole in the floor, Casey would have crawled into it. Then Abbot called on Casey.

Rising, he began: "A lawyer should be an orator, but I don't make any more claims along that line than I do to being a hero. I appreciate all this tonight." He put a finger under his collar and tried to stretch it, suddenly aware that there were tears in Lola's eyes. "Folks, I just did what had to be done, and I'm glad I was there to do it."

They cheered.

Casey waited for quiet, and went on: "We all know what a bank means to a community. Credit is the life blood of business." He paused and took a drink. "I don't need to tell you about the place Mister Scoggins and his bank hold in this community, but I do want to say something that will interest all of you. I understand from the sheriff that a reward of five thousand dollars is coming to me. I intend to turn it over to the community to add a room to the schoolhouse and to hire another teacher. I hope there will be enough left over to build a gymnasium."

They gave Casey a tremendous ovation. Scoggins clapped lightly, twice, green eyes suspicious as he waited for the rest of what Casey had to say.

"I regret that some cultural advantages are lacking," Casey went on. "As you know, we need a library. I am afraid, however, that my contribution will not be enough, so I hereby challenge Mister Scoggins to come to our assistance, matching dollar for dollar what I give."

Silence. Mrs. Scoggins was the first to recover. She prodded her husband with a sharp elbow.

Scoggins was very pale when he gripped the table and pulled himself upright. "I'll do it . . . we've got to encourage culture." He sat down and wiped a hand across his brow.

No one cheered. Everyone but Casey was too shocked to believe what they had heard.

Abbot said: "Well, Ed, here's another surprise. We wanted to show our appreciation, so we took up a purse for you." He handed a heavy bag of money to Casey. "There's two thousand dollars for you, contributed by the businessmen of San Rafael."

Casey rose again. He paused while he gathered his thoughts.

"Folks, this is mighty generous of you. I'd like

your permission to add this money to the reward. With Mister Scoggins doubling it, you will have fourteen thousand, enough to give us the finest library in the county . . . along with enlarging the school and adding a gym."

More cheering, but not so loud. Everybody had heard too much. It was like looking at a plate of candy after filling up on cake. There was dancing afterward, but the Scogginses excused themselves and went home. When Casey had a chance, he asked Abbot: "Why isn't Julia here?"

"She's smart, Ed. She wouldn't come. Anyhow, you don't need her. Eli can't back out now."

Casey grinned. "He'll try."

Casey drove directly to Lola's boarding house after the dance. He helped her down, and she took his arm as they walked up the path to the house. She had been strangely quiet after they left the lodge hall. Now she stood with her back to the door and looked at him.

"It was a generous thing you did tonight, Ed," she said, "and the way you handled Scoggins was miraculous, but there's something else that's more important and I want you to know it. It's wonderful to have an example like you in a community that has had too much Scoggins."

"Not as wonderful as having you for a teacher," he said. He drew a deep breath. "Lola."

"Yes?"

"Lola . . . will you . . . marry me?"

63

She lifted her lips to his, murmuring: "Of course, Ed."

He kissed her, knowing beyond all doubt this was what he wanted.

"You've got to know," he said, "I'm no part of a hero."

"Oh, Ed, it's you I love. Just be who you are." Then she shivered in his arms. "I'm afraid, Ed."

"Of what?"

She did not answer for a long moment. "People's memories are so short."

III

Casey drove back to Mrs. Davis's, telling himself he should be the happiest man in town. He was going to have the prettiest wife in San Rafael. Lola was respected and liked by everyone. Abe Rucker would say Ed Casey was a fool for luck. He was. He knew he was. That was the thing that bothered him.

Lola hadn't known she'd loved him until he gunned down the Potters. After a while the glamour would wear thin. Where would he be with Lola then?

He stabled the bays, seeing a light in the parlor and thinking Mrs. Davis had left it there for him. But when he came in, he saw Mrs. Davis sitting on the edge of her chair and Eli Scoggins in the loveseat over in the corner, his thin face as sour as clabbered milk.

Casey controlled his surprise. "Howdy, Eli. That was a fine thing you did tonight."

Scoggins made a noise in his throat and sat as if he were paralyzed, green eyes as sharp and as wicked as chipped class.

Mrs. Davis said uneasily: "Mister Scoggins has been waiting to see you for an hour."

Casey dropped into a chair. "I noticed you left the shindig early. I was afraid you were sick."

Scoggins made another noise in his throat. He turned to Mrs. Davis. "I want to talk to Casey. Alone." He added: "And no eavesdropping."

Mrs. Davis rose, red-faced. "Eli, you ought to be ashamed."

Casey spoke after she sailed out of the parlor. "You should be ashamed, Eli. What do you think she's been sitting up for?"

"I am not here to exchange pleasantries," he said. He paused. "Casey, you surprise me."

"I've been surprised a few times myself today."

"I thought at noon when you played hero that it was a case of being in the right place at the right time. You have practiced law in San Rafael three years, but without spectacular success. I will say people like you well enough, especially around deer season."

Casey eyed the banker, wondering what was coming next.

"I had classed you with Abbot and Rucker and the rest," he went on. "Now I see I was wrong. You caught my weakness as accurately as you shot the Potters. I cannot stand ridicule or public disgrace, even if it costs me seven thousand dollars." He went on: "There is another queer thing about what you did tonight. I can afford the loss of seven thousand dollars, but you can't. I daresay you haven't made that much since you hung your lawyer shingle out."

"Let's say I have principles, Eli."

"There's only one basic principle beneath all human actions, Casey. We do things or don't do them according to how much they benefit us. The extra teacher and the gym and library don't mean a damned thing to you except that they'll make people notice you and thereby bring more business to you. Today luck was beating you on the head. Everybody has noticed you. You'll have more business than you want. And you've got Lola Horn. So we can forget all of this civic improvement nonsense."

"Afraid not, Eli. I said I had principles. I meant it."

"Oh, hell," Scoggins said in disgust. "That's a public show. This is between you and me. We can get out of this if we work together." He added: "I'll make it worth your while."

Casey felt like laughing in his face. "You're wasting your time."

66

"There are other considerations beside the financial ones," he said. "There's talk of making you mayor. I would go further. Say a seat in the legislature."

"Not interested." Casey rose. "Deer season opens tomorrow, Eli. I've got to get some sleep."

Scoggins came to his feet. "I never threaten a man, Casey, but your attitude leaves me with only one course of action." He paused. "I know how to destroy you. All the ammunition I need is right here."

"You scare me, Eli. Good night."

Scoggins rose, picked up his hat from the walnut table, and walked out.

Despite tough words, a vague uneasiness burned in Casey. He'd had his choice of peace or war, and he'd picked war. Maybe he was a fool. In a showdown men like Lou Abbot and Abe Rucker would give him no help.

Casey stepped into his room, struck a match, and lighted the lamp on his bureau.

"You keep late hours, Mister Ed Casey."

He wheeled, the lamp chimney in one hand, the burning match in the other. Julia Larson was sitting on the bed, laughing silently. The match burned his fingers. He cursed and dropped it, stepping on it immediately as he thought of what Mrs. Davis would say if she found a hole in her carpet.

First he slipped the chimney into place. Then

he locked the door. "What are you doing here?"

"Do you have to lock that door to keep Missus Davis out?" she asked.

"She just might sail in if she heard a woman's voice in here," he answered.

"I'm not worried about my reputation," she said, smiling. "Maybe you are about yours."

"Maybe I am," he said. "Do you usually go around getting into men's rooms at night?"

"Not often," she replied. She added: "Just when they're town heroes."

He dropped into a chair and filled his pipe. He had known Julia Larson only casually. She had given him some legal business, and he had danced with her a time or two. She was a very striking woman, blonde and a little plump, but not too much so. Her blonde hair was rumpled as if she had been lying down while waiting for him. Her pale green dress was low-cut, her skirt too short by San Rafael standards.

She rose and shook her dress into place, and, when she sat down again, she drew her skirt higher.

He asked: "How'd you get in?"

"Window," she said.

He said: "From now on I'll have to lock it to keep beautiful women out."

"You won't have to worry about this one," she said. "I didn't suppose you were so straight-laced."

"I got myself engaged tonight."

"Engaged? Not that black-haired teacher?"

"That's right."

She shook her head in disgust. "Ed, I thought better of you than that."

He struck a match and sucked the flame into the pipe bowl. "Jealous?"

"Sure," she said with a laugh. "You're a big man."

He liked the way she laughed. She rocked on the edge of the bed, hands clasped around her knees.

"What did you come for?" he asked.

"Business." Her full red lips tightened as she studied him. "Ed, I want to thank you for inviting me to the shindig tonight, but it's like I told Abbot. I don't belong to San Rafael's version of society. I want something else out of life, and I'm going after it."

"What?"

"Wealth and independence," she said. "And I want to hammer Scoggins." She asked: "What was he doing here tonight?"

"He wanted me on his side."

She laughed again. "I don't blame him. I want you on my side, too."

"How did you know he was here?"

"Saw him go in before I climbed in through your window." She asked: "Did you say yes?"

"Nope."

"That makes you my kind of man, Ed. That's why I'm here."

Julia rose and moved toward him. He started to rise, but she motioned for him to keep his seat. She stood before him, looking down and breathing a little hard. Lola had never affected him this way. It was like receiving one electric jolt from Julia after another.

"A lot of people wonder how I've been able to hold up against Scoggins," Julia said. "Mostly it's because I have financial backing outside. The Yankee Boy is a good mine. I've got enough ore blocked out to keep me going for years. My trouble right now is I've bitten off more than I can chew. Last week I bought all the claims on the hill. I own it all now."

She moved back. "Scoggins would give his eye teeth to get his hands on my property. He just may do it, too. Those crazy prospectors who owned the claims I bought demanded cash. I had fifteen thousand dollars brought in secretly on the stage."

She paused. "I can't prove it, but I think Eli Scoggins sent for the Potter brothers."

Casey stared at her, pulling on his pipe. It just might have been that way. He remembered Scoggins saying that, if Fred Bent had kept his mouth shut, he wouldn't have been shot. And when Casey had suggested Scoggins wanted his bank robbed, the banker had flashed anger.

"It would have looked good," Julia went on, "Scoggins saying my money was handy and in the hurry the Potters didn't take anything else. No one would ever know he divided it up with the outlaws."

"But they didn't get it," Casey said. "So you're all right."

"No, I'm not. I've paid for the claims, but now old Poley Gibbs who owns the toll road down the mountain has jumped his rates. Most of my ore is low-grade, so I operate on a pretty small margin. I suppose Scoggins put Poley up to it. Anyhow, the only thing I can do is buy Poley out. Ten thousand, he says. Cash."

"Can you raise it?"

"Sure, but it's got to be here tomorrow. Scoggins won't loan it, so I've got to bring the money myself. I'm afraid to do it. Pete Ennis won't give me any protection. Ed, if I don't have the money tomorrow, Poley swears he'll make a deal with Scoggins. Then I'm finished."

Casey knew Poley Gibbs by sight, a tough, loud-mouthed old man who spent most of his time drinking in San Rafael saloons.

"What can I do?" Casey asked.

"You mean you're on my side?"

"Sure."

"What will Lola say?"

"I don't know."

She moved closer, dropped down on his lap, and put her arms around his neck. "I'm driving an ore wagon to the bank at Cotter's Junction tomorrow. I want you to ride shotgun."

"Julia, I'm a lawyer."

"No, Ed. You're the town hero who shot three outlaws as neat as if you'd been cutting cake. News like that goes out over the Owlhoot Trail fast. With you on the seat beside me, I won't have any trouble. Will you do it?"

He was uneasy, not from the prospect of danger, but wondering about Lola. He said: "Sure."

She kissed him and jumped up. "We're leaving at six." Crossing the room to the window, she added: "Don't worry. I won't tell Lola."

IV

Casey got up at 5:00 a.m., dressed, and wrote a note telling Mrs. Davis he wouldn't be there for breakfast. He left the house, taking his Winchester, had breakfast at the Top Notch Café, and got to the stage depot at five minutes before six. Julia, clad in a man's shirt and Levi's, was pacing nervously around the big wagon.

"You had me worried, Ed," she said as he came up. "I was afraid you'd get to thinking about Lola and go back on our deal."

He said with some sharpness: "I don't go back on a deal."

"Let's roll," she said, and climbed to the high seat.

It was said around San Rafael that Julia Larson could do anything a man could. Now, watching her handle the ribbons, Casey agreed. They wheeled into Main Street and five minutes later were out of town and starting down the long grade to the railhead at Cotter's Junction.

Lola cast a sidelong glance at him. "You sure Lola's the woman for you, Ed?"

He nodded. "Don't you like her?"

"You know how it is with me," she answered. "Nobody in San Rafael invites me into their homes. Lola will fit that pattern. She'll give teas and parties, and she'll be a social asset to you." She added: "If you want to live like that."

"Guess I do," he said.

"I would have agreed up until yesterday noon," she said. "Now I think you're fooling yourself. You're made to live tough. Maybe you'll die young, but not before you've had a hell of a good time."

"I'm not that way. I haven't changed just because . . ."

She laughed. "You're really fooling yourself now. Up until yesterday you were a lamb like Abe Rucker and Lou Abbot. Now you're a hell-roarer and you'll never be the same again."

He didn't believe it. Circumstances had pitched him into a position where he could challenge Eli Scoggins. He would have done the same any time in the past.

"You're wrong, Julia. I haven't changed."

She gave him a quick, penetrating glance.

"When we get back to San Rafael, you'll find out. Either you'll bow and scrape like the rest of them, or you'll keep on being a hell-roarer until Scoggins is licked." She stared down the twisting road, her face suddenly bleak. "I set out to be a hell-roarer and I can't back up. Know why I'm black-balled?"

"No."

"It's Missus Scoggins's tongue. Eli's idea, of course. He thought that was the way to get me out, but I'm stubborn. So I've done without the things most women think are important. No husband and no home and no kids. I've had to fight off the men I didn't want, and the men I like treat me like poison."

"If you went somewhere else . . ."

"I won't, Ed. I'm not made that way." Her lips tightened. "When a woman debases her pride, she hasn't much left, but that's what I'm going to do now."

Casey looked at her.

"If you ever decide Lola isn't the woman for you," she went on, "I'd like to try to fill the bill."

This was something he hadn't counted on. He stared ahead, knowing he had to say something and failing to find the right words. He finally said: "Thanks, Julia."

"Now you forget it," she said with forced lightness. She added: "Unless the time comes to remember."

There was no more talk until they reached Cotter's Junction. The heavy box was passed up and slid under the seat. Two men on horseback watched. Before Julia climbed back up to the seat, she said loudly to the agent: "What do you think of my guard, Phil?"

The agent squinted up at them. "Who is he?"

"Ed Casey."

"The fellow who shot up the Potters in San Rafael?" he asked.

"Yep!"

On the road back, Julia laughed and said softly: "That pair watching us will think twice now before they start anything."

Casey looked back. They were not followed. He watched every turn in the road, every tree, and every boulder, Winchester held on the ready. They reached town before noon without trouble.

They wheeled down Main to the bank, chain traces *jingling,* dust rolling up behind them. Julia drew a long breath. "We're here, Ed, but I don't think I'd have made it if it hadn't been for you. If there's ever anything I can do to help you out, let me know."

"Forget it," Casey said.

There was a crowd in front of the bank, Abbot and Rucker and Sheriff Pete Ennis, and a few others. Casey stepped down and walked over to Abbot. "I figured you'd be out after your buck this morning."

"Not today," he said sullenly.

Something was wrong. He looked around the half circle, feeling their hostility. Scoggins hurried out and the box was carried inside. Poley Gibbs was on hand, acting disappointed and saying he hadn't thought Julia could raise the *dinero*.

After she had gone inside with Gibbs and Scoggins, Casey asked: "What's the matter with you boys? This looks like a wake."

"It is," Rucker said. "The wake of a hero."

"I don't get it," Casey said.

"You ought to get a rope," Rucker said. "Yesterday you're walking high and handsome and you propose to Lola. Word is, she said yes . . . because she doesn't know what you are. She knows now."

Casey grabbed a handful of Rucker's shirt front. "You'd better keep talking, Abe."

"I'll talk, all right. You couldn't wait, could you? You promise Lola, and that same night you have this woman in your room."

It soaked in then. He knew what Eli had meant with that comment about destroying him. He had seen Julia, too.

Casey hit Abe, knocking him off the walk into the street. "Put that in your paper."

"That didn't buy you anything," Lou Abbot said. "You're finished in this town. You can't buy us. We don't want the money you were giving away last night."

"You sure as hell don't have to take it," Casey said. "You don't even know the truth."

"You're denying Julia came to your room, Ed?" Ennis demanded.

"I'm denying nothing," he said.

"I happen to love Lola," Rucker said, "and I don't aim to see her treated this way."

"That's right," Ennis said. "We'd run you out of town if you had more than five minutes to live."

"What're you gents talking about now?" Casey demanded. "A lynching?"

"We're talking about Duke Dorsey," he replied. "Go get your gun. He's waiting for you in the Idle Hour Saloon."

V

Julia had come out of the bank in time to hear what Ennis said. She pushed past Abbot. "Don't do it, Ed. This is Scoggins's work."

"I reckon it is," Casey agreed, "but these boys seem to favor the idea. Yesterday I was the first citizen. Now Eli is."

Julia said: "That's the way the men of San Rafael are."

"Two of a kind," Ennis said with a sneer. "She's your woman, all right, Casey."

Anger built a fire in him. He hit Ennis, battered him back across the walk, and knocked him headlong into the bank.

He turned to the others. "If you had any sense, you'd see that you're playing Scoggins's game."

Ennis was on his feet, one eye swelling. "You're hell with your fists, Casey, but too yellow to face Dorsey."

"You're hell for shooting a bunch of running men, too," Rucker added, "but you haven't got what it takes to face Dorsey."

"Have you?" Julia asked.

"Shut up." Rucker bit back another word he would have called her.

"Or you, Sheriff?"

"He isn't after me," Ennis answered.

"But you'll sit still and let him murder a man," Julia said angrily. She swung to face Casey. "You aim to do it, don't you?" she asked.

Casey's gaze swung around the bunched men, his face bone-hard. Yesterday he had been a hero; today he was a tramp.

"There's a sort of code, Julia, like in the days of old when men dueled. There isn't another man here who'd do what this bunch expects me to do."

"Then what difference does it make what they think?" she demanded.

"None," Casey said. "I don't know any reason why I should be killed because these cowards call me a coward."

Without another word he swung away from them and slanted across the street. He passed the front of the Idle Hour Saloon and turned the corner.

He remembered Lola. She had said people's memories were short. To hell with the bunch of them. Scoggins had done a perfect job. He'd proved he understood these men better than Ed Casey had. He had fixed it so they would make a pariah out of him, the way his wife had shunned Julia.

School was out. Kids were moving away from the schoolhouse. Lola would be along in a minute. He turned down a side street and waited. Soon he saw her coming in her graceful stride. She lifted a hand to him and waved, hurrying her steps.

Casey took off his hat and held it at his side, with the same hand that held his Winchester. "Have you heard the gossip about me?"

The smile froze on her lips. "Why do you ask?"

"I've got to know."

Her eyes searched his. "Yes, I heard. Does it make any difference?"

"There is one thing that makes all the difference. Do you believe it?"

"Yes. I believe Julia was in your room. Abe Rucker is a truthful man. But I won't believe you did anything wrong unless you tell me yourself."

A great breath came out of him. In that moment he knew that only Lola's opinion was worth anything, that the rest of San Rafael meant nothing by comparison. He had Lola's love, and that was enough.

"I never heard anything in my life that meant more to me than what you just said." He took her hand. "Whatever happens, believe two things. I did not do anything wrong. And I love you."

He let go of her hand and wheeled away, walking rapidly to the alley. He turned there and came into the Idle Hour through the rear door.

There was no one in the saloon but the barkeep behind the mahogany bar and Duke Dorsey on the customer side. He was a tall, long-necked man with a leathery face and a pair of blue eyes that were on Casey from the moment he entered.

"You're Dorsey?"

"That's right," the gunman answered.

"I hear you're gunning for me," Casey said, cocking the Winchester.

Dorsey edged away from the bar. "Where's your Forty-Five?"

"I don't own one. This will do."

Dorsey looked shocked. "Go get a real gun."

"This will do," he repeated. He added: "You're a fool for taking Scoggins's money to kill a man you never saw before."

"A thousand dollars," Dorsey said, "makes a good day's wages."

"All right. Earn your money."

"Not with you holding that Winchester on me. Go get a handgun and fight like a man."

Casey moved one step to the side and put the Winchester on the bar. "Now it's as far from my hand as that Forty-Five is from yours. Make your play."

"The hell I will," Dorsey said, and turned away, heading for the door.

Dorsey took two steps, halted, and swung back, drawing his gun. Casey had expected treachery and had grabbed the big rifle. He fired once, just ahead of the Colt .45. Dorsey's face twisted. He dropped his gun, grabbed at his shirt front, and fell.

Casey ran past the dead man into Main Street. The crowd was moving slowly toward the Idle Hour, led by Rucker and Ennis. They stopped and stared.

Doc Miller broke the silence. "Did he hit you, Ed?"

"No," Casey replied. He added to Rucker: "Tough luck."

Casey went past them to the bank. Then Lola was at his side. He didn't know where she had come from. He only knew she was there, holding his arm and trembling as she clung to him.

"I'm all right," he said. "I've got business with Scoggins. You go on now."

"I'll stay with you, Ed."

He grinned. She walked beside him to the bank. The crowd followed at a distance. Casey glimpsed Julia coming out of the hotel, angling toward them.

Casey found the banker at his desk. He stepped

through the gate at the end of the railing. Scoggins saw him and rose.

"Good scheme, Eli, but it backfired. Dorsey's dead. Now you've got me to contend with."

The banker's mouth sagged open. "This doesn't concern me."

"You're wrong, Eli. Dorsey said you paid him a thousand dollars to kill me."

"He's lying."

"Barkeep heard it all. You're done in this town."

"Keep threatening Eli," Ennis called out behind him, "and you'll find yourself behind bars!"

"No, you won't," Julia said. She came through the crowd and stood beside Lola. "It's time somebody took care of Scoggins, and I'm picking Ed Casey to do it."

Some of the townsmen started toward Casey. He turned, his Winchester at the ready. "Stay there, Pete."

Julia turned to the townsmen. "There's something you boys need to know. A while back Scoggins used the bank's money to speculate on mine properties. He lost, and I quietly helped him out to keep the bank from going under. Now I own a chunk of this place, a big chunk." She smiled. "And you can be sure I'll straighten Eli out."

Scoggins wiped a hand across his face, looked at Casey, then at the men out front. They were obviously shocked to learn of the misuse of funds. Pete Ennis was no help now.

Julia turned to Scoggins. "Well?"

"All right, Julia," he said, "all right."

"From now on this bank will be operated in good faith," she announced. "With honesty."

Casey strode to the sheriff. "Resign, Pete. Resign, or I'll yank that star off your shirt myself."

Without a word, he pulled it off his shirt, threw it at Casey, and stomped out. Rucker gave a last look at Lola, and followed.

"Well, Ed," Julia said, "this bank partnership will take some legal paperwork. Can you do the job?"

"As soon as I take Lola back to school," he said with a smile.

Julia turned to her. "I made a mistake about you. I thought you were all milk and toast. You know, silk and ribbons and foofaraw. But you're a hell-roarer, like me and Ed."

Puzzled, Lola said: "I don't understand."

"Ed will tell you," Julia said, holding out her hand. "He's a good man."

Lola took her hand. "I've got to get back," Lola said, and turned to Casey.

They walked into the street, Lola holding her head high, a hand on Casey's arm. Lou Abbot was waiting outside with Doc Miller and some others.

Abbot asked: "When are we going deer hunting, Ed?"

That was the way they were. When a man was

on top, they were with him, and right now Casey was up there. But he couldn't forget.

He said curtly—"Not this fall, Lou."—and went on with Lola.

When they were out of earshot, Casey said: "You changed yesterday after the Potter business. I'm not a hero. You've got to remember that. After everything settles down . . . I mean . . ." He floundered, searching for words.

Lola said: "You're trying to say that I suddenly became too forward after you made yourself San Rafael's number one citizen."

"No, I mean . . . well, you had been kind of offish."

"You might remember, Mister Ed Casey, that you are the chairman of the school board. Perhaps you weren't aware of it, but you always acted very official. Second, after the shootings, I knew you'd need some support." She added: "And as far as the rest of the single men of this town are concerned, I don't want any of them."

Ed Casey stopped and turned to face her. "I never thought of it that way. Will you accept my apology?"

"I'll forgive you," she said, adding: "There's one way you can fix it."

He leaned closer and kissed her there on the street where all could see them.

THE DURANGO STAGE

I

Ollie Dutton stood on the steps of the coach as the engine rolled past the Alamosa depot, a long, indistinct shadow in the uncertain dawn light. He heard the *clanging* of the bell and the *growl* of brakes, then the car jerked to a stop. Ollie swung down to the cinders along the track and strode rapidly toward the stagecoach standing at the end of the depot, a suitcase in one hand, a locked leather bag in the other.

" 'Morning, Mike," Ollie said to the driver as he set his suitcase down. "How long have I got till you're pulling out?"

Mike McCoy, the driver, peered at Ollie in the vague light, then he said: "Oh, it's you, Ollie. You get what you went after?"

So McCoy knew, Ollie thought. By this time it was probably all over Durango that Ollie Dutton had gone to Denver to raise $10,000 and he'd be bringing it back if he had any luck. Well, he should have known. Men were bound to talk about a deal as big as this one, especially in a town the size of Durango.

"Well, I'm back as you can see," Ollie answered, "and I've got to be in Durango before noon Monday, if that tells you what you want to know."

McCoy laughed softly. "It does, Ollie, it sure does, though I'd better warn you that we may have a hell of a tough time getting there. You've heard about the pack of outlaws that's operating between here and Durango, but maybe you ain't heard we've got a band of renegade Injuns on the prod, too."

"No, I hadn't heard that," Ollie said. "Utes straying off the reservation?"

"I reckon one or two might be Utes," McCoy said, "but the agent claims they're mostly Paiutes who have drifted in from Utah. The trouble is they know some of the Utes and they jump back onto the reservation if it gets too rough and hide out there. But don't worry about getting back in time. This is Saturday morning. We'll have you in Durango Sunday night if we have any luck. We're carrying a heavy treasure box along with that *dinero* you're toting in that little leather bag."

"Who's riding shotgun?"

"Al Ash. He's a good man."

"I know," Ollie said. "Well, you haven't told me how long I've got."

"Oh, half an hour," McCoy said. "Meet the stage at the hotel if you've got other business."

"I'm going to try to talk Jean Mason into going back with me," Ollie said. "That may take more'n half an hour."

"Well, for a pretty girl like Jean," McCoy said, "I'll hold the stage a little longer."

"Thanks," Ollie said, and strode past the depot toward the main street.

Folks in Durango knew just about everything about everybody, Ollie thought as he moved through the near darkness, and that included his quarrel with Jean. They'd been engaged for six months, and they would have been married by now if he'd kept on working for the Animas River Syndicate, but, no, he'd got himself involved with his two best friends, Pete Risley and Duke Warren, in the Katydid Mine.

Ollie wouldn't have made the deal if he'd known what was going to happen, but how could any man guess what a woman would do? No, that was just an alibi and it was time he quit thinking it. He should have foreseen this.

He knew Jean had her heart set on a June wedding, and he knew she had a hair-trigger temper, so it didn't take any big brain to figure out that she'd jump the traces when he told her he had put all his money into a long-shot gamble on the Katydid and they'd have to postpone the wedding until September. The instant he said that, she jerked off her ring and gave it to him, locked up her millinery shop, and took the next stage to Alamosa where her parents lived.

Now Ollie needed her, but that wasn't the reason he was going to her. She hadn't been gone from Alamosa five minutes until he knew he loved her far more than he had realized. He didn't have any real hope she'd take his ring back and return to Durango with him. She'd probably be so mad at him for waking her up at this hour that she'd slam the door in his face.

When he reached her house, he saw a light in the back. Her father was a cattle buyer. Probably he was up before daylight, planning to get an early start on a long trip.

Ollie knocked on the front door, his heart slugging in his chest.

The door opened. She stood across the threshold from him, peering into the dawn light. He heard her whisper—"Ollie."—as if she couldn't believe it was he, then she screamed—"Ollie!"—and threw herself at him, hugging and kissing him and saying between kisses: "Ollie, I didn't think you'd ever come."

She pulled him into the house and led him on back into the kitchen, then stood looking at him, her blue eyes shining. He set the leather bag on the table and took her into his arms and kissed her again. He was six feet tall and she was barely five, so she always had to stand on her tiptoes to kiss him. Now she stepped back and put a hand up to her blonde hair, suddenly embarrassed.

"I must look a sight," she said. "You've got no right to call on your girl at this time of the morning. I just got up and started the fire." She paused, and then asked in a low tone: "Ollie, have you still got that ring? I've felt naked ever since I gave it back to you."

Vastly relieved, he laughed shakily as he drew his wallet out of his pocket and, taking the ring from it, handed it to her. He said: "I've carried it with me all the time just to have it handy in case you came back."

She slipped the ring onto her finger and held it up for the diamond to catch the lamplight, then she looked at him and giggled.

"I couldn't do that, Ollie. A girl can't go to the man after they've had a fight. He's got to come to her. It's what you did, isn't it?"

He nodded. "That's exactly what I did. I asked Mike McCoy to hold the stage and I told him I was going to try to talk you into going back with me. I can't give you a June wedding, seeing as this is July, but I will give you one as soon as we can find a preacher."

"That's exactly the offer I've been waiting for." She hesitated, fixing her gaze on his face. "Ollie Dutton, is there a joker in this deck?"

"Yes and no," he said. "That's something I want to talk about. I've got a job I want you to do, but it might be dangerous and I've got no right to ask it. Fact is, it's even dangerous to be on the stage."

She shook her head, smiling. "Sure, a wheel can come off or the horses can run away. I guess there's some danger just getting up in the morning and walking across the room. The roof might fall in."

"This is more than that," Ollie said. "Mike McCoy says we'll probably be fighting off outlaws and Indians before we get to Durango. Whether you do the job or not, I want you to know that I love you and I was a fool to let you leave Durango in the first place. We'll get married whether I have a nickel in my pocket or not. That is, if you want to."

"Of course I want to, but you'd better tell me what I'm supposed to do." Her face turned red as quick temper boiled up in her. "Has it got anything to do with the Katydid?"

"Sure it has," he said. "I'm not going to lie to you about that, but will you listen to me before you blow up and hand the ring back again?"

For a moment she fought her anger, then she shrugged her shoulders. "All right, I'll listen, and then I'll marry you, and after that I'll cut you down to size every time you start chasing some crazy will-o'-the-wisp like the Katydid Mine. The way a man gets ahead is by being steady and working hard, and not gambling on something all the time." She flushed as if realizing she was nagging him. "Ollie, you know how it's been with us. Ma and I have starved most of our lives because Pa was out buying and selling cattle, and losing money more often than he made any."

"There's something I tried to tell you before

you left Durango," Ollie said. "Pete and Duke and me have been friends since we were kids. Now they both need a stake. Pete's wife has got to have an operation and she's got to go to Denver for it. Pete says it'll cost a fortune. Duke's got five kids with another one on the way. He just couldn't make it working for the Syndicate."

"But you were the one who put up the money to lease the Katydid," she said. "It was a long chance, taking over a mine that the Syndicate had given up on."

"Sure it was a long chance," he admitted, "but you win some big pots playing poker that way. Anyhow, we were lucky. We've blocked out more than one hundred thousand dollars' worth of ore. We agreed to keep it a secret, but Duke gets gabby when he drinks and the chances are he drank too much after I left Durango. Billy Bellew and the rest of the Syndicate boss men know by this time what happened. We can figure on them doing anything including murder to keep me from getting back with the money to buy the Katydid."

Ollie patted the leather bag. "I raised ten thousand dollars in Denver. That's what it takes to buy the Katydid. That figure is in the contract, so we're all right that way, but we've got only until Monday noon to deliver the money. If it isn't in Judge Lorne's office by that time, the mine goes back to the Syndicate."

She thought about it a moment, then shook her

head. "Ollie, I know you're not lying to me. All three of you are experienced miners, so you wouldn't make a mistake, but the Syndicate had given up on the Katydid. They hadn't brought anything but country rock out of that tunnel for months. Everybody knows that."

"Sure," Ollie agreed, "and we likewise know that the Syndicate took a fortune out of the Katydid before they lost the vein. Well, Billy Bellew has run the Syndicate from the time it was organized. He's mean and greedy, but he's smart, too. He figured it wasn't worth spending their time and money trying to find the vein, but he was willing to let us try on the chance we'd find it but couldn't raise the money to buy the mine from them. In other words, he gambled on getting some free work done."

Jean looked down at her hands, and said in a low tone: "I'm sorry, Ollie. I'll do whatever you want done, and I'm not afraid of outlaws or Indians."

"Good girl," he said. "But you'd better find out what I want done before you make any promises. Have you got a shoe box, one that would look like you were carrying a lunch in it?"

She nodded, disappeared into her bedroom, and came out a moment later with a shoe box that looked the worse for wear. She asked: "Will this do?"

"Perfect," he answered. "Where's your folks?"

"Visiting Sis in Del Norte," she said. "I didn't

want to go. Ollie, I might as well admit it, I'm a shameful hussy. I was going back to Durango. I couldn't wait any longer for you to come after me."

He grinned at her as he unlocked the leather bag. "Well, then, it's a good thing I got here. Is it all right just to go off and leave the house?"

"Oh, yes," she answered. "The folks will be back this afternoon. I think they expect me to be gone." She turned away. "After all, I am twenty-one and an old maid. It's time I was married."

He lifted several packages of money from the leather bag and laid them on the table beside the shoe box. He knew she would be glad to leave home permanently, for Jean had never been happy here.

"I'm in the same fix you are." He grinned. "I'll be an old man if I don't get married and settle down. I don't want to put it off any more. I know now we should have gone ahead and got married in June the way you wanted to even if I was broke."

He fitted the packages of money into the bottom of the shoe box, then said: "Now I want you to fix some sandwiches. Anything. Bread and butter will be all right. Smear a little butter on the lid. Lay a napkin or something over the money, put in a layer of sandwiches, another napkin, some more sandwiches, and cover them with a napkin. That will fill the box. Put the lid on and tie a string around the box, then hang onto it all the way to Durango."

"And this is dangerous?"

"It might be," he said, "when you're dealing with a man like Billy Bellew. The stage will be held up. You can count on that."

He dipped into the leather bag and showed her a package of money. "This is a stack of ones with a hundred dollar bill on top. I've got five of these. I'm risking over five hundred dollars that's in this bag on the chance they'll take it and ride off without paying any attention to the lunch box."

"Oh, you are a foxy one," she said. "I'd better get started making sandwiches or Mike won't hold the stage for us."

He stood at the table watching her fill the shoe box with sandwiches. There wouldn't be any danger to her, he told himself. She'd be riding in the coach safely beside him, holding the innocent-looking shoe box on her lap. Still, he was uneasy. He knew the uneasiness would last until the money was in Judge Lorne's office and the papers were signed and the Katydid actually belonged to Ollie Dutton and his partners.

II

Ollie knew that time was getting away from them. As soon as Jean looped the string around the shoe box, he said: "We've got to hurry."

She nodded as she finished with the knot. She ran into the bedroom, changed quickly into a dark blue traveling suit, put on a trim white hat, and carried her suitcase into the front room where he waited for her. She blew out the lamp and they left the house, the shoe box in Jean's hands, Ollie carrying his leather bag and Jean's suitcase.

Ollie walked rapidly, Jean having to run to keep up with him. Worry nagged him until they rounded a corner and he saw the stagecoach waiting in front of the hotel.

"Get a move on," McCoy said irritably. "You're holding us up. I wouldn't have waited another thirty seconds even for a pretty girl like you, Jean."

"I'm sorry," Jean said as McCoy took her suitcase and stowed it in the boot. "I had to change clothes and pack. I didn't really expect to go this morning."

"I had her fix a lunch," Ollie added. "I can remember a time or two when I needed a lunch on this stage."

"We'll make it to Rome's by noon," McCoy said, his voice still cranky. "Climb in."

Al Ash, the shotgun guard, stood beside the front wheel, a Winchester in his hands, a Colt .45 on his hip. He asked: "Got plenty of shells for that iron you're packing, Ollie?"

Ash was about McCoy's age. Both men were younger than Ollie, but neither was reckless. In this country the reckless usually died young. Ollie guessed that McCoy and Ash had filled men's boots for the last ten years, and he had complete confidence in both.

"Plenty," Ollie answered. "Trying to scare Jean?"

Ash laughed softly. "No. I just thought she ought to know that this is going to be a rough trip."

"Shut that talk up," McCoy said roughly. "We'll make it. Ollie, want me to toss that leather bag into the boot?"

"No, I'll keep it with me," Ollie answered.

Standing close to Ollie, McCoy said in a low tone: "Watch that fellow named Horn. I don't trust him worth a damn." As he wheeled toward the front of the coach, he said in the same cranky voice: "Get in. You've held us up too long now."

Ollie gave Jean a hand as she stepped into the coach. By the time he followed and had pulled the door shut, McCoy was in the high seat, the lines in his hands. The silk sailed out over the horses and *cracked* with pistol-like sharpness in the chill morning air; the horses leaned into their collars, and the big coach rolled down the street.

Jean and Ollie sat facing the direction they rode. A dark-haired girl was beside Jean, and three men sat across from them. Ollie knew Ted Conner, a middle-aged man who had a pig farm a mile downriver from Durango, and he also recognized Johnny Roan, a young fellow who had done everything from punching cattle to working in the mines. According to gossip, he had been friendly with the outlaws that plagued Durango, although Ollie had never heard of Roan's being arrested.

Ollie spoke to Conner and Roan and extended his hand to the third man. He had not, as far as he could remember, ever seen the man before. He said: "I'm Ollie Dutton. I guess we'd better get acquainted, seeing as we're going to be together for a spell."

"Of course," the man said pleasantly as he shook hands. "I'm Ed Horn. I've heard of you. The story is you're about to make a deal for the Katydid and you're carrying the purchase price of ten thousand dollars."

"There's a lot of gossip in this country," Ollie said more sharply than he intended. "Don't believe all you hear." He nodded at Jean. "My fiancée, Miss Jean Mason. Jean, I guess you know Johnny Roan and Ted Conner."

"I know Mister Conner very well," Jean said. "I made two hats for Missus Conner just before I left Durango." Conner nodded and mumbled something about them being good hats. Jean looked at Johnny Roan. "I don't believe I have met Mister Roan."

Johnny's freckled face broke into a wide grin. "I sure know you, Miss Jean. I used to walk past your shop just to look at you. You were that pretty."

"Hold on, Johnny, hold on," Ollie said. "She's my girl."

"Well, I'll tell you one thing," Johnny said. "You aren't gonna keep other men from looking at her."

"That's right," Horn agreed. "You are to be congratulated, Mister Dutton."

Jean turned to the girl beside her who had been listening with quiet amusement. "They are all filled with blarney this morning, Miss . . . ?"

"Norton," the girl said. "Sally Norton. I'm going to Durango to marry Lieutenant York. He's stationed at Fort Lewis. Do you know him?"

"No," Johnny Roan said, "but I hate him. I've got two days before you meet him and I'm going to make you forget him."

"Really, Mister Roan, you are not all you think you are," the girl murmured. "The lieutenant has no need to worry."

"Wait and see," Johnny said smugly. "By tomorrow night I will have you in my clutches."

"Heaven help you, Miss Norton," Jean said.

The girl turned to Jean. "You're right. Heaven help me if I ever get into his clutches."

"I was just talking foolishment," Johnny said, suddenly serious, "but if your lieutenant isn't on hand when we get to Durango, and, if you need anything, just let me know."

"I never saw the day I couldn't take care of myself, Mister Roan," the girl said, and turned to the window as if letting all of them know she wanted to be let alone.

Ed Horn had been watching and listening, and now that the talk had died down, he said: "Mister Dutton, I want you to know something. I am a man of many talents. At the moment I'm on my way to Durango to work for the Animas River Syndicate. Of course, Billy Bellew doesn't know it, but he will. One of my talents is my ability to sell myself to men like Billy Bellew."

"You've never met him?"

"No, but that doesn't make any difference," Horn said cheerfully. "He'll hire me. A man smart enough to run an outfit like the Animas River Syndicate is smart enough to know a good man when he sees one."

Ollie was amazed by Horn's arrogance, but he might be right. Ed Horn was a smooth and handsome man, probably around thirty, neatly dressed, but no part of a dude. He was not wearing a gun in a holster as Ollie and Johnny Roan were, but Ollie judged he had one or more on him.

Horn was not a big man, perhaps five feet nine inches tall, and he would not weigh more than 160 pounds, but somehow he contrived to give the impression of bigness. He was soft-voiced and courteous, yet there was an unyielding steel-like quality that made Ollie wonder if he had been a professional gambler. For all of his apparent courtesy, Ollie had the conviction he was a very tough man.

"Maybe Bellew will hire you," Ollie said after a pause. "He's smart. I'll say that for him."

"That brings me to what I wanted to say," Horn went on. "This deal for the Katydid is no concern of mine. I don't aim to try to stop you or take your money." He motioned toward the leather bag. "If Bellew wants to know why I didn't put a crimp in your plans, I'll plead ignorance of the whole business."

"I'll appreciate that," Ollie said.

They were out of town now, the last gray adobe shack behind them. The coach was running full tilt across the flat floor of the San Luis Valley, the barren land reaching for miles all around them. The saw-tooth crest of the Sangre de Cristo range was behind, the great bulk of the Blanca Peak heaving up against the sky. Ahead of them were the San Juan Mountains. If the day went well, McCoy should have the coach over the top and well down the other side by dark.

Daylight had deepened; the long shadows that had danced ahead of them with the first of the sunrise had now begun to shorten. The smell of dust was in the air along with the tangy scent of sage and pine, indicating that it had rained recently somewhere ahead of them. Heavy black clouds still hung above the San Juans. Ollie guessed they'd be in a thunderstorm before they made their night stop.

Leaning back, Ollie closed his eyes. Jean's head rested sleepily on his shoulder. He heard the *creaking* of the coach, the *groaning* of the leather braces, and the steady *thud* of hoofs against the dust of the road. He wondered why McCoy suspected Ed Horn instead of Johnny Roan.

Later, when McCoy rolled the coach into the yard of the first stage station, Ollie stepped down long enough to ask in a low tone: "Why Horn instead of Johnny?"

"I seen Horn with Bronc Killion last night in Alamosa," McCoy answered in an equally low tone, "and Killion was a friend of Billy Bellew. I reckon he still is."

Ollie nodded, suddenly sick in the pit of his stomach. The horses were changed; the coach rolled out of the yard and headed straight toward the great, dark barrier that was the San Juan Mountains. Now Ollie was really concerned about Ed Horn. Bronc Killion had indeed been a friend of Billy Bellew's before he went bad.

The outlaw was supposed to be somewhere in New Mexico with his wolf pack. He wouldn't have come back to Colorado if he hadn't been on the trail of something worthwhile. The something could very well be the $10,000 that was in the shoe box on Jean's lap.

Jean, awake after the brief pause at the stage station, looked at Ollie and asked: "You feel all right, honey? You look kind of bilious."

"That's it," he said. "I'm bilious."

He leaned back and closed his eyes again, remembering the days when Bronc Killion had been his friend, too, his and Pete Risley's and Duke Warren's.

III

Bronc Killion and his men rode into the yard of Abel Rome's road ranch in the middle of the morning and ordered Rome to give the horses a double bait of oats. He led the way into the log house and told Mrs. Rome to get dinner for them, then he paced impatiently back and forth across the big room as he waited to be served.

For a time Bronc stood in the doorway, staring moodily down the road. Here and there he could see patches of the valley floor and he wondered how far away the stage was. Would Dutton be on it as Ed Horn had assured him? He knew one thing. He'd be damned sore if Ollie Dutton wasn't on it.

Holding up the stage and robbing a single man was one thing, especially a man Billy Bellew was paying them to rob. Taking the treasure box was something else. He didn't want the stage company on his tail and that's exactly what he'd have if he took the strongbox. But if Dutton and his $10,000 weren't on the stage, Killion would have a hard time keeping his men from taking the box. They'd figure they had earned something for the morning's work.

"It's ready!" Mrs. Rome called.

Chino Lopez grunted something about its being about time as they sat down at one end of the long table. The others were silent as they began to eat with wolfish appetite. Shorty Armand and Pig-Nose Rafferty were too old and tired even to grunt, Killion thought as he helped himself to the venison roast, but Larry Engel wasn't a man to waste anything, even a grunt.

Funny the kind of men you throw in with when you have to, he reflected. He'd recruited the four of them after he'd left Durango. Chino Lopez was part Mexican and part Anglo, and probably a big part Indian, although he wouldn't admit that. He was only twenty, more animal than man, Killion often thought, with his wide jaw and narrow forehead. He was worse than a stud horse. A woman meant only one thing to him, a weakness that was going to get them all into trouble one of these times.

Shorty Armand and Pig-Nose Rafferty were run-of-the-mill owlhooters you could find any time you landed in an outlaw hang-out. They were both about fifty and had served time in half a dozen prisons. They claimed they had ridden with Jesse and Frank James and the Younger boys, and Killion guessed they were lying in their teeth.

Larry Engel was a different breed of dog. He

was thirty, Killion's age. He was mean and smart, and ambitious as hell. He wanted a lot of money —he never had told Killion why—and he didn't give a damn how he got it. He was the only one of the four with a brain in his head, and Killion was just a little afraid of him.

So far they hadn't hit the jackpot, but if they did, Killion had a hunch Engel would try to gun him down and take over the outfit, then divide the money with half for himself and an even split of the rest for the other three. Killion had an idea they'd take it lying down.

They were more afraid of Engel than he was, and Killion knew he'd better beat Engel to the draw if they ever hit it big. One thing Killion had learned since he'd started riding the Owlhoot—it paid to play his hunches.

The Rome girl came into the dining room with the coffee pot and filled their cups. Killion watched Chino Lopez, saw the gleam in his dark eyes, the half smile on his lips, and suddenly Killion was furious.

The instant the girl disappeared into the kitchen, Killion said: "Forget it, Chino. Forget it right now. You won't get us into trouble on account of a girl if I have to cut your damned head off."

Lopez nodded and grinned, his white teeth gleaming. "*Sí, señor,*" he said.

"Cut it out," Engel said sourly. "You can talk American as well as anybody."

Lopez grinned at him and nodded. "Sure, boss."

"Damn it, Bronc's the boss," Engel said. "Not me. What're you trying to do?"

"Nothing," Lopez said. "Just stay out of trouble. That's all. I don't want no trouble with nobody."

That was Lopez for you, Killion thought. He'd drag a girl out into the brush any time he had a chance. He'd shoot a man down whether he had an excuse or not. He'd put his knife blade into a man's belly in a saloon over some fancied insult, but he'd look you right in the eyes and tell you he didn't want trouble with anybody.

Killion glanced at the Seth Thomas pendulum clock on the wall and saw that it was 11:30 a.m. "Time we got out of here," he said as he rose.

Killion laid a gold eagle on the table and turned to the door. He paused in front of the mirror to admire himself, thinking of the fine clothes he'd worn in Durango, of the comfortable room with its featherbed he'd had in Mrs. Lauder's house, of the parties he'd taken Jean Mason to, of the girls on the line in Durango who thought he was all man.

At times he became sentimental when he remembered the good life he'd had in Durango. He'd been Ollie Dutton's friend then. Pete Risley's and Duke Warren's, too. And Billy Bellew's. Oh, yes, Billy Bellew's, by all means. He guessed he was still Bellew's friend or the great man wouldn't have sent Ed Horn after him.

Chino Lopez was halfway to the door when he

wheeled and walked back to the table and picked up the gold eagle and dropped it into his pocket. The other three had left the house. Apparently Lopez thought that Killion was so busy admiring himself in the mirror that he wouldn't notice.

"Put it back," Killion said wearily. "Chino, someday I'm going to beat you to death for your thieving ways."

Lopez spread his brown hands. "Why throw away good money, *amigo*? The women, what have they done to earn it? Me, I need it for poker."

"Put it back," Killion said.

For a moment Lopez stared at Killion, stubborn and resentful, then he grinned his white-toothed grin and shrugged his shoulders. "*Sí, señor*," he said.

Lopez dug the coin out of his pocket, laid it on the table, and walked out. Killion went back to the table and saw that Lopez had left the eagle. It would have been like him to substitute a silver half dollar. He was tricky, Killion thought angrily, tricky enough that he couldn't be trusted when the blue chip was down if he had a chance to rake in the blue chip himself.

The others were mounted when Killion joined them. Abel Rome was watching them from the corral gate. Killion asked: "When does the stage get here?"

"Twelve," Rome answered, "give or take five minutes when the weather's good."

"Don't tell 'em we were here," Killion said. "It would spoil the surprise."

"You figure they'll be surprised?" Rome asked.

Killion laughed as he stepped into the saddle. "Maybe not," he said as he reined out of the yard.

From Rome's place the road climbed and twisted into the pines. They didn't hurry; Killion knew they had more than an hour. He took the lead, thinking again of the good days in Durango and the satisfaction he'd have in cutting Ollie Dutton down to size.

Killion had had the inside track with Jean Mason, or so he had thought. He'd taken her buggy riding; they'd gone to parties and dances, and he never doubted that all he had to do was to ask her to marry him and she'd say yes without a moment's hesitation, but that was before Ollie Dutton began paying any attention to her.

He didn't suspect that Ollie had fallen in love with Jean, although he had known Ollie was spending some time with her. When she finally told him that she was marrying Ollie, Bronc couldn't believe it. She told him plain out that as far as she was concerned, they were just good friends.

He'd made a fool out of himself then. His pride had been hurt; he couldn't let her go just like that. He swore at her and said she'd never marry Ollie and took her into his arms. He'd show her he loved her and then she'd know she loved him.

He kissed her, hard and long, in spite of the kicks and pounding she gave him. The next thing he knew Ollie had him by the shoulder and yanked him around and hit him on the jaw, a hard wallop that knocked him flat on his back.

Killion tried to make a fight out of it, but that first punch took it out of him. It ended up with him getting the worst beating he'd ever taken in his life. Later, when he'd had time to think about it, he'd told himself that maybe he had been wrong in making her kiss him, but he'd never had a woman treat him that way before. He was a favorite of all the girls on the line, he told himself. He didn't consider Jean any different from them.

Not long after his fight with Ollie a couple of men had come to him with word that the stage was bringing in a heavy treasure box. Why not take it, they'd asked. What the hell, he'd told himself, nothing here for him now. So they'd tried and failed, with Al Ash cutting the other two down. Bronc got away with a bullet gash in his left arm. But Ash and McCoy had recognized him, and within forty-eight hours Reward dodgers for him were hanging all up and down the San Juan and Animas Rivers.

He wouldn't be back in Colorado now if Bellew hadn't sent word by Ed Horn about the $10,000 Dutton would be carrying, and that he'd pay another $10,000 if Killion prevented Dutton's returning to Durango with the money to buy the

Katydid. It was too good a deal to pass up, so here they were.

He wondered how he'd feel when he faced Al Ash with a gun in his hand. Dutton, too. He'd want to kill both of them, but he wouldn't. Adding murder to the robbery would only make things worse. Besides, Bellew had said no shooting.

A few minutes past 12:00 p.m. they reached a sharp curve just above a steep climb with huge boulders on both sides of the road. "This will do," Killion said as he reined up and dismounted. "They'll be moving slow when they hit this curve. Get the horses off the road."

He handed the reins of his big bay to Shorty Armand and climbed to the top of a tall boulder near the road. He thought he could see a dust cloud far to the east. Maybe the stage was just now pulling into Rome's. He slid back to the ground just as the other four returned from hiding the horses and settled down to wait.

IV

The stage pulled off the road and wheeled into the Rome yard two minutes before 12:00 p.m.

"Noon stop!" McCoy called as dust made a brief white cloud around the coach and gently drifted away and men ran from the corral to take the horses.

McCoy swung down and strode toward the barn.

Ollie stepped out and gave Jean a hand, then helped Sally Norton to the ground. Horn, Roan, and Conner followed. Jean and Sally moved toward the house, Jean clutching the shoe box as if she were afraid someone would try to take it from her. Al Ash stood beside the coach until McCoy returned, then he went to the barn.

For a moment McCoy was silent, his gaze on the pine-covered foothills and the high pass that was not far to the west of them and shook his head. "I wish we were on the other side. That's where they'll hit us if they're going to."

"We'll make it," Ollie said.

"Sure." McCoy grinned. "We'll go ripping through them hills just like a knife through hot butter. Well, let's go see what kind of chuck Missus Rome has got to put on the table today."

Ollie walked with McCoy to the house. As the girls opened the door, Johnny Roan, running from the barn, called: "Hold on, Sally! I want to sit beside you. It'll make the grub taste better."

She stopped and looked at him, then she said in a cool, distant voice: "Well, if gall could make food taste better, sitting beside you would certainly give it a fine flavor."

"Sure would," Roan said, not at all abashed. "It's better'n salt or pepper or horseradish."

"Just about the same as horseradish, I'd say," Sally remarked scornfully.

Jean smiled as she sat down at the long table

beside Ollie. "She told me she would have taken the next stage if she'd known Johnny Roan was on this one," she whispered.

"She can handle him," Ollie said. "It strikes me she's enjoying his attention."

"The lieutenant may not enjoy it when we get to Durango," Jean said.

The Rome girl came in with a dish of gravy and a plate of biscuits and set them on the table.

"Well, Linda," Johnny Roan said, "you get prettier every time I see you."

The girl flushed and fled back into the kitchen. "At least you're impartial," Sally Norton said. "I guess you spark all the girls."

"Of course," Johnny said. "You never know where lightning will strike, but you are my one true love."

Sally sniffed and made a point of ignoring him after that. All the men had come in, Al Ash sitting so that he could watch the coach through the open door, his Winchester leaning against the wall directly behind him.

Mrs. Rome swept into the dining room with a platter of venison steaks. "Eat hearty," she said in her booming voice. "You won't get nothing to eat at Pa Finley's place tonight. Nothing that's fit to eat, I mean. Nobody's there to cook now but the girls."

"Sounds like professional jealousy," Ollie said.

Mrs. Rome paid no attention to him. She had

seen the shoe box on the table beside Jean's plate and said indignantly: "Well now, Miss Mason, I like that, fetching your lunch when you knew you'd be here for dinner."

"I didn't have any way of knowing I'd be here for dinner," Jean said. "With Mike McCoy driving, I didn't think we'd get five miles out of Alamosa."

McCoy had just taken the platter of meat from Ed Horn. He held the platter in his left hand, the fork in his right ready to spear one of the steaks. "By grab, Jean," he said, "I hope it's snowing when we get on top because you'll be the first to get out and walk."

"I trust your driving, Mike," Jean said, "but after all the talk about Indians and outlaws and such, I didn't think any of us would get through."

Abel Rome had just come out of the kitchen with the coffee pot. He stopped dead still and stiffened, his stubble-covered face turning pale. He asked hoarsely: "What's this about outlaws?"

"Idle gossip, Abel," McCoy said. "Just idle gossip. Jean's pulling my leg, but I'll wait my turn to pull her leg."

"There aren't any outlaws around here," Rome said vehemently, a pulse pounding in his temples.

Rome set the coffee pot on the table and wheeled and left the dining room. In that instant something changed. Everyone ate in silence except to ask for the meat or potatoes or gravy.

Jean ate half of her steak and pushed her plate back, refusing even to take a piece of pie when it was passed. Ollie glanced at Sally Norton. She was frightened, too, although Ollie doubted that she knew why.

Abel Rome had disappeared into the kitchen. He had been so scared he walked with a strange, jerky motion. This wasn't like him, Ollie thought. Rome had operated this stage station from the time the line had been put through to Durango and Ollie had never seen him upset about anything.

Fear, Ollie knew, was contagious, and Abel Rome had just started an epidemic. Even McCoy and Ash were uneasy. Ash's gaze was fixed on the coach. As soon as he ate his pie, he rose, picked up his Winchester, and left the dining room. Only Ed Horn seemed to be untouched by this strange current that had swept around the table. Horn helped himself to a second piece of pie and glanced up as if wondering why the others had quit eating.

Ollie leaned back and rolled a cigarette. The chances were that all of them had heard about the outlaws being in the country. With the possible exception of Ed Horn, they had been uneasy from the time the stage had left Alamosa and it had only taken Rome's vehement statement that the out-laws were not around here to start the epidemic.

Rome knew that outlaws were close or he wouldn't have said what he had in the way he had said it. The only questions were how close were they and what were their plans. Ollie wasn't sure Rome knew the answers, but he aimed to find out.

They got up from the table a moment later, Ollie carrying his leather bag and Jean tucking the shoe box under her arm. She glanced at him and tried to smile, but she couldn't quite manage it.

"Quit worrying," Ollie said out of the corner of his mouth.

"Oh, I'm not worrying," Jean said. "Not one bit more than you are."

Ollie grinned. "You got me," he said. "Right between the eyes." He turned to McCoy. "Hold up a minute. I want to see Rome."

"One minute," McCoy said. "If you're longer than that, you can walk."

"I'm not figuring on walking," Ollie said, and strode toward the barn.

Abel Rome had picked up a fork and had started to clean out the first stall. When he saw Ollie, he shouted: "Get to hell on that coach, boy! McCoy's got fresh horses and he's ready to roll."

"I know," Ollie said as he patted his leather bag. "Abel, you've heard the story about why I went to Denver and you know why I'm going back and why I've got to be in Durango by noon Monday. It seems that everybody knows it."

Rome nodded. "I've heard it, but if you don't . . ."

"You likewise know how far Billy Bellow will go to keep me from getting to Durango," Ollie went on, "and you know that Bronc Killion was Bellew's friend. Now where is he?"

"I dunno," Rome said, turning surly. "It would serve you right if Mike drove off and left you."

"It isn't just me and the Katydid Mine that's involved," Ollie said. "There's two women on that stage and I'm aiming to marry one of them. I don't want them hurt and I don't think you do."

Rome straightened up. He jammed the fork into the litter at his feet and glared at Ollie. "What good will it do if I tell you what I know? You won't turn around and go back to Alamosa, so they'll hold you up just the same."

"Then they were here?"

Rome nodded. "Five of 'em. Killion is the only one I knew, but they're a bunch of mean bastards."

"How long ago were they here?"

Rome considered the question, then he said: "I didn't look at my watch, but I'm guessing they left about an hour ago."

"Thanks," Ollie said, and turned toward the barn door.

"Don't tell 'em," Rome begged. "For God's sake, don't tell 'em I opened my mouth to you or they'll come back and murder all of us."

"I won't," Ollie said, and walked rapidly back to the stage.

The passengers were inside. McCoy and Ash were on the high seat, Ash's rifle between his legs. Ollie stopped to say in a low tone: "They'll hit us in less than an hour if I'm guessing right."

McCoy nodded. "I figured that's the way it would be. Abel was scared right out of his shirt. They must have stopped here."

"Let's not make a fight out of it," Ollie said. "I don't want the women hurt." He patted the leather bag. "This isn't worth it and neither is the treasure box."

"How many of 'em?" Ash asked.

"Five."

"I'm not promising nothing," Ash said. "It all depends on how they work it. I'll start shooting if I figure I've got a chance."

"You won't have," Ollie said. "By now Killion's an old hand at the game. He'll play it like a professional."

Ash nodded agreement. "You're probably right. There's a dozen places between here and the top where they can stop us and we won't have a chance."

"Get in," McCoy said. "We're rolling."

Ollie stepped into the coach and shut the door as the big coach wheeled out of the yard and into the road and headed west. All of the passengers looked at him as if expecting him to tell them something.

Ollie leaned back. He said: "I knew Abel didn't feel good the way he looked. I asked him about it. He says his stomach is giving him fits."

Ed Horn was amused. "Funny," he said, "I thought the grub was good."

"I thought so, too," Ollie agreed, "but maybe Abel's just got a touchy stomach. How'd you like the grub, Sally? Did that gall you were talking about help flavor it?"

"No," she said.

For once Johnny Roan didn't grin or have a smart remark to make. They rode in silence as the coach started to climb. Ollie had told himself he had not caught the fear that had flowed out of Abel Rome. The hold-up was exactly what he had expected and he had planned for it. His scheme would work. They'd take his leather bag and ride off and that would be the end of it.

Then he wondered why he was trying to fool himself. His heart was skipping every third beat and his stomach felt as if he had swallowed a stone for dinner.

V

Bronc Killion glanced at the sun every four or five minutes. When it seemed about time for the stage to appear on one of the sweeping curves, he climbed to the top of the tall boulder again and studied the road below them. He saw a cloud of dust, and presently the coach appeared around a turn, moving slowly because of the steep slope.

Killion estimated that the coach would take another ten minutes to get here. He slid back to the ground and said: "It's coming."

He studied the four men, noting the expression of apathy on the faces of Shorty Armand and Pig-Nose Rafferty. This was a familiar situation to them. Most of their old partners were dead, usually ending their lives by standing on nothing and swinging from the end of a rope. They would probably follow the same route, or die with lead in their belly. This was their way of life; they would follow it to the bitter end, and Killion knew he could count on them.

Larry Engel was different. He had no intention of dying. He wanted money, all he could get and as soon as he could get it. He hungered for the power and the status money would give him, and Killion had a hunch he wanted a reputation. The James boys. The Youngers. The Daltons. He'd overshadow the lot of them in time. Still, he was smart, and he'd play the game until he figured the time was right for him to take over. That would be later, not now.

Chino Lopez was the one who worried Killion. He wondered as he had a good many times why he had ever taken the young whelp into the outfit. Lopez was like Engel in one way. He wanted money, but only because it would buy women, or get him into a poker game or buy a fine horse and a silver-studded saddle. His problem was one of sheer stupidity. He simply wasn't smart enough to figure things out if the hold-up did not follow the plan.

"I'm going to tell you exactly what to do and I expect all of you to do what I say," Killion said. "We want the *dinero* Ollie Dutton is carrying. That's all. We'll divide the money, equal parts for the five of us. If we pull this off, we go to Billy Bellew and he gives us another ten thousand that we divide equally."

"What do you mean *if* we pull this off?" Engel asked in his lazy way.

"I mean somebody in this outfit may get other ideas," Killion said. "Like robbing the stage company of the treasure box. We don't want the damned company putting a bunch of detectives on our trail and chasing us to hell and gone. We're not robbing the passengers, either. It wouldn't amount to enough to fool with. Just Dutton." He pinned his gaze on Lopez. "You savvy, Chino?"

"Sure." Lopez spread his brown hands. "I do just as you say."

"If you don't, I'll shoot you," Killion said. "That's a sure promise. Just as sure as the sun's coming up in the morning."

Lopez's white teeth gleamed. "I am scared, boss. I am scared very bad."

He was an animal, Killion told himself, a stupid

animal. He motioned to a boulder at the edge of the road that could be rolled by four men. "Get it out here," Killion said. "Just far enough to stop the stage."

The others moved behind it and after a few grunts and curses turned the rock over so that it occupied half of the road next to the base of the tall boulder Killion had climbed. There was not enough room for the stage to get around it.

"Good." Killion nodded as he took a red bandanna from his pocket. "Larry, you and Chino get up there where I was. Cover your faces. Have your guns in your hands, but don't shoot unless they start it. I don't think they will because they're dead ducks if they do and they'll know it."

For a moment Killion's eyes locked with Engel's and he sensed that the other outlaw had recognized the same danger from Lopez that he had. He could, he thought, count on Engel to keep Lopez from doing the wrong thing.

"Shorty, you and Pig-Nose get on the other side of the road," Killion said. "Stay under cover till I give you the sign. When the time's right, I'll have 'em throw down their guns. You two pick 'em up and carry 'em up the road fifty yards or so. Put 'em down where they can find 'em. They may need 'em pretty bad before they get to Durango."

Armand and Rafferty nodded and disappeared into the brush on the opposite side of the road. "Larry," Killion said to Engel, "find a small rock you can toss at me when it's time for me to show."

Engel nodded and, stooping, picked up a small rock and put it into his pocket. He and Lopez had tied their bandannas over their faces. Now they climbed to the top of the boulder where they dropped on their stomachs and lay motionlessly, revolvers in their hands.

Killion hugged the uphill side of the boulder, his bandanna covering his face, his Colt in his right hand. This was the moment for which he had been waiting, and yet his heart was sledging away in his chest as if it were about to break out.

He couldn't be as offhand about this as Armand and Rafferty were. Killion knew that Mike McCoy and Al Ash were on this coach and he wanted to kill them, Ash in particular. He felt the same way about Ollie Dutton because Dutton had beaten him unmercifully, but not as much as he did about Al Ash. Ash had given him a painful wound and killed his two friends, and he would never feel right until he had squared accounts with the man. But all of this would have to wait, he told himself.

He heard the *rumble* and *squeak* of the big coach and the *rattle* of trace chains; he heard a man swear and another man speak to the horses, then the stone dropped on his shoulder. He called: "Hook the moon! Unless you want to die, don't start shooting. Four guns are lined on your briskets." He stepped into the road, his cocked .45 in his hand.

McCoy and Ash were on the high seat, Ash's rifle in his hand ready to fire. But he didn't pull the trigger. Killion guessed Ash had seen Engel and Lopez on top of the boulder and he may have seen Rafferty and Armand on the other side of the road. In any case, Ash fought and conquered the impulse to cut Killion down.

"Good," Killion said. "Guard, ease the hammer down on your Winchester and toss it on the ground. Both of you do the same with your revolvers, then get your hands up like I told you to." McCoy and Ash obeyed and lifted their hands. "Now you passengers get out, slow and easy. We're not here to kill anybody. Obey orders and nobody gets hurt."

The door opened and Ollie Dutton stepped out, a leather bag in his hand. He was a fool, Killion thought contemptuously, to carry the money on him. It might be a decoy, of course. If so, he could have the money on him or hidden in the baggage. Killion doubted that it was in the strongbox.

Now Killion's heart began to thump and dip and he could hardly believe his eyes. He saw Dutton hold up a hand and help Jean Mason to the ground. Killion had supposed she was still in Durango. He had no idea why she was in the stage now headed toward Durango, but it didn't make any difference. She was here in the flesh.

He watched her as she moved forward until she stood in front of the horses. She was a little bedraggled from long hours of travel in the coach, but to Bronc Killion she was a very pretty, graceful woman. The only woman he had ever loved, he told himself, and certainly the only woman he had ever wanted and had not possessed.

Ollie Dutton followed the two women, then three other men got out of the stage, and the six of them lined up along the road. Killion remained motionless, staring at Jean, wanting her so much that he came very close to changing the plan and taking her along.

Engel said: "Looks like he's carrying the *dinero*, all right."

The words shocked Killion back to the reality of the moment. He was surprised at himself. He had gone over this scheme carefully in his thoughts, planning out every move, and yet now he had been so shocked by Jean's appearance that he had stood there like a man in a trance.

"Open the bag, Dutton," Killion said.

For a moment Dutton glared at him as if he were going to refuse. He said: "I've got to take this money to Durango. It means a fortune to me and my partners. I'll pay you off later, double the amount that's here."

"Unlock it," Killion said wearily. "I'm not here to argue about it or listen to you beg. If you can't find your key, I'll cut it open with my knife. You can be damned thankful you're alive. Try to stay that way."

Dutton moistened his lips with the tip of his tongue, hesitated another second, then he shrugged as if he understood he had no choice. He fumbled in his pocket, found the key, and unlocked the bag. Killion took it, glanced inside, and saw that there were five packages of money, each bill one hundred dollars. Then he snapped the bag shut.

"Drop your guns," he said, his eyes running along the line from Johnny Roan and Ted Conner to Ed Horn. For a moment his gaze lingered on Horn's face, but the man showed no hint of recognition.

It seemed to Killion this was easy, too easy, but of course there was nothing Ollie Dutton could do. He had always been an open-handed, kindly man, honest and frank, and something of a sucker in Killion's eyes. If anything was wrong, Ed Horn would tip him off.

The revolvers dropped into the dust, then Horn said as if he were very angry: "We're a long ways from Durango. We'll need those guns if the Indians are raiding like we hear."

Killion motioned for Armand and Rafferty to come out of hiding. They appeared, picked up the guns, and carried them up the slope. Ash called from the box: "For God's sake, don't set us up for pigeons! That renegade bunch of Paiutes is hunting easy scalps and you know it."

Killion motioned toward the man on the boulder. "Get the horses." He stepped forward and jerked the shoe box out of Jean's hands. He saw terror turn her face pale and he found a great deal of satisfaction in knowing that she was afraid of him. He promised himself that there would come a time when she would be more afraid of him than she was now. He'd ride into Durango some night after dark and he'd find her and he'd have her and she would never forget him as long as she lived.

"It was right kind of you to fetch a lunch for us," Killion said.

Her lips quivered and for a moment he thought she would not be able to say anything, then she blurted: "I fixed that lunch for myself. I've ridden this stage before and I've been hungry. I didn't want to go hungry again."

He broke the string that was tied around the box and took the lid off. He grabbed the napkin that covered the sandwiches, threw it to the ground, took a sandwich and bit into it.

Jean cried: "Please! You've got what you want. Do you have to make me go hungry?"

Engel and Lopez had led the horses into the road. Killion started to chew, then spat the mouthful out, and threw the sandwich to the ground.

"Butter," he said in disgust. "My God, a bread and butter sandwich!"

For a moment he held the box as if he were going to empty it onto the ground, then he changed his mind and shoved the box at her, bumping her roughly in the stomach. He wheeled away, dropping his gun into the holster, and swung into the saddle.

"You'll find your guns up the road a piece," Killion said. "You might need 'em for the Indians at that. Just stay where you are until we're out of sight."

He rode upslope, Lopez and Engel leading the other two horses. They reached Armand and Rafferty who mounted and fell in behind Killion. A moment later they turned off the road and headed down the side of the mountain toward the willow-lined creek in the bottom of the cañon. Somewhere, sometime, Killion told himself, he would possess her. He had to.

VI

For several minutes the passengers standing in front of the stage and Ash and McCoy in the high seat remained motionless until Bronc Killion's gang had disappeared from sight, and then suddenly Jean began to cry. Ollie took her into his arms and the tension was broken.

Johnny Roan began pacing back and forth, cursing as if he had gone crazy. He wheeled and shook his fist at Ash, bawling: "You had your Winchester. You could have smoked that bastard down. Why didn't you do it? You're yellow. That's why."

126

Ash swung down off the high seat, saying furiously: "I'll show you who's yellow!"

Conner and Horn stepped between the two men, but it was Sally Norton who silenced Roan. She moved forward and slapped him across the side of the face, a sharp, cracking blow, then she said: "I'm not used to listening to that kind of language and I'm not going to listen to it now."

He shut up. He raised a hand to the side of his face and stared at her blankly, apparently unable to remember what he had been saying or doing. Ollie released Jean who had stopped crying, the shoe box clutched so tightly under her arm that it was crushed in the middle.

"You'll have to forgive him, Sally," Ollie said. "He's about out of his head." He gave Roan a push. "Go pick up our guns. Conner, give him a hand."

Conner nodded, understanding. "Come on, Johnny. They aren't far up here."

Roan started up the road, stumbling and reeling as if he were still only half conscious. Ash looked at him and shook his head. "I don't savvy this. What's he so jumpy about?"

"I was wondering that, too," Horn said. "Seems like it should be Dutton, but he's standing here as cool as a cucumber."

Ollie suddenly realized he wasn't behaving in the way a man would who had just lost $10,000 and a fortune with it, and that it was time for him to do some play-acting. He said: "I guess I'm still dazed, Horn. It'll hit me later. Right now I feel like Killion said we should, lucky to be alive."

"That's the truth," Ash said. "As soon as I seen that rock in the road, I knew we were in for it, and the next second I seen them two on top of that tall boulder. And when Killion sang out for us to hook the moon, I looked at them two guns pointed down my throat, and I figured that they'd let me have it the first wrong move I made."

"There's something else maybe you didn't know, Horn," Ollie said. "Killion's sweet on Jean. One time after we were engaged I caught him kissing her. She was kicking and hitting him for all she was worth, but he had her in a bear hug. I yanked him around and he let her go and I beat hell out of him. I lost my temper and maybe I shouldn't have been so hard on him. Just now, when I stood here looking at him, I was thinking I was gonna pay for it."

"I was afraid he was going to make me go with him," Jean said.

"I'll bet my bottom dollar he was thinking about it," Ollie said. "Well, Horn, I lost a fortune, but I've got my girl and we're all alive. Maybe it wasn't such a bad bargain after all."

Horn nodded, his narrowed eyes fixed thoughtfully on Ollie. "I guess we are all lucky at that."

Ash was staring up the road at Roan and Conner who had reached the guns and were picking them up. He said: "Funny how your mind works at a time like this. I knew you'd whipped the bastard, and I knew he'd been sweet on Jean, but I was thinking about the time I'd stopped the first hold-up he tried. I wounded him and rubbed out his two pals. I figured that all he needed was an excuse to smoke me off that seat."

"Now that you've gabbed a while," McCoy said irritably, "how'd you like to move the rock?"

"Looks purty big to me," Ash said.

"Well, try, damn it," McCoy said. "We can't get around it. You'll either build a new road or we'll set here forever if you can't move it."

"Might be easier to move it than build a new road," Ollie said.

The three men got behind the rock and heaved, but they couldn't move it an inch. It not only was big and heavy, but it was so smooth they couldn't find any handholds. Finally they stood up and shook their heads at McCoy.

"No use," Ollie said. "Looks like the ground was slanted a little where it was in the first place. That's how they were able to move it, but now it's in the hole and the slant's against us."

"No use waiting for the others," Ash added. "No more'n three men can push on it to do any good."

"We can't get hold of it, McCoy," Horn said. "That's the main trouble."

"Get me the axe," Ollie said. "I'll cut a pry among those saplings yonder."

He walked off the road into the spruce trees, looking for one that was small enough to handle and still would do the job. Ash joined him a minute later and handed the axe to Ollie as he said in a low tone: "I don't know what kind of a sandy you pulled on Killion, but I figure you fooled him some way. Maybe gave him counterfeit money. The thing I want to know is whether Horn swallowed what you said."

Ollie found the small spruce that he was looking for. He chopped it down and trimmed off the branches. He said finally: "I made a mistake. I should have done some cussing and dancing around the way Johnny was doing. That's what everybody expected of me, but I didn't think of it. I saw how Killion was looking at Jean, and all I could think of was that the bastard was going to take her with him and there wasn't a thing I could do to stop him."

"I thought of that, too," Ash said, "but now I'm wondering whether Killion will try again. If he does, when will he hit us, and will Horn back him?"

"Nothing to do but wait and see," Ollie said. "It won't take 'em long to find out they got the short end of the stick, then I suppose they'll be back. Next time they'll go over everything with a fine-toothed comb."

He finished and handed the axe back to Ash. When he carried the pole to the rock, Roan and

Conner were there with the guns. Ash said harshly: "You called me yellow, Roan. You want to back that remark up now?"

"No." Roan swallowed and glanced obliquely at Sally. "I apologize if that does any good. I guess I was out of my head. I thought they'd gun us down. Then I figured they'd take the girls. After they rode away with Dutton's *dinero*, I kept wondering why we didn't unhook the horses and start after 'em."

"We couldn't have caught 'em," McCoy said. "I wouldn't have let you do it anyhow. They aren't my horses. Besides, my job is to get this stage through to Durango. Now, damn it, Ollie, see what you can do with that rock."

Ollie shoved the tip of the pry under the rock and with Horn's and Conner's help lifted the opposite end. The rock barely moved. They tried again and once more it moved a little. After that it was an inch by inch process until they reached the shoulder of the road. By that time the big rock was out of the hole from which it had started. The men gave it one final push that rolled it on over into the brush.

"It's about time!" McCoy yelled. "Get in. We've lost half an hour now. Maybe more."

Ollie took his gun from Roan and slipped it into his holster. Ash was already sitting beside McCoy, his rifle resting on his knees. The girls went inside the coach. As soon as the three men were in and the door closed, McCoy's whip *cracked* and the horses leaned into their collars. The heavy coach *creaked* and *groaned* and once more started the laborious climb to the summit.

Ollie held Jean's hand and Sally Norton looked out of the window, her face pale as she tried to see the bottom of the cañon. Ollie wondered if her lieutenant would ever understand the price she had paid to join him. Or, for that matter, did he understand what Jean had just gone through? And they weren't done with this by a long shot.

He didn't mention his worry until the middle of the afternoon when they reached the steepest part of the climb. McCoy stopped to blow the horses and called: "This is a good place to stretch your legs!"

The six passengers got down and walked up the road. The stage remained where it was for a few minutes, then passed them. Jean reached for Ollie's hand and squeezed it. As they walked, she said: "I never knew that a few seconds could seem like a lifetime, but the few seconds I stood looking at Killion after he grabbed the box was a lifetime."

She took a long breath, glancing at the cañon below the road. Ollie, watching her, thought she didn't see the meandering stream far below them or the tall spruce trees growing in the bottom of the narrow valley and looking like tall, green spears from this point. Her mind, Ollie thought, was still on those terrifying moments when she had stood beside him, the guns of Killion's men pointed at them.

"I never want to go through that again," she half whispered.

"I don't want you to, either," Ollie said. "It didn't seem like I was asking you to do much back in Alamosa, but when we were standing on the road with five guns lined on us, I wondered how I could ever have been such an idiot."

"Well, we're all right so far," she said. "I've got a hunch we're going to be all right, too."

"I've been thinking." Ollie glanced at her, not at all sure he could convince her to do what he wanted her to. "We'll get to Finley's place about half past six or seven. You'll be safe there. I want you to stay till the next stage comes through."

She turned to him, her mouth open. "Ollie Dutton, I will not do any such thing. I guess this sounds crazy, but I don't want to be separated from you again."

"It doesn't sound crazy," he said, "but now that we've been through this much, I know I couldn't stand it if anything happened to you. For a little while when I was so sure he was going to take you with him . . ." He stopped and looked ahead at Sally Norton and Johnny Roan, then he said: "Jean, I want you to stay there at Finley's."

"Ollie, did you ever stop to think that with this Paiute renegade bunch in the country, I'd be safer with you in the stage than staying there at Pa Finley's place?"

"I don't see how you figure that."

"You know the kind of man Finley is. You also know he never keeps more than two men. That adds up to three, counting Finley. With just the girls, well, if the Indians attacked his ranch, they'd get burned out and probably everybody would be murdered."

It was hard to argue against that. She was right. He knew what she meant when she said "the kind of man Finley is." The saying along the stage route was that he was too light for heavy work and too heavy for light work, so he hired two men and started an overnight stage stop. He plain just wasn't any good.

When Ollie remained silent, she glanced at him, her lips squeezed together in grim determination. "Ollie, I'm going with you to Durango."

He nodded and didn't push it any longer. He knew from experience that when she had this determined expression on her face, there was no use to argue.

VII

Bronc Killion sat his saddle, his gaze fixed on the slash high above them that scarred the side of the mountain. It was the road to Durango, and the stage was on that road and Jean Mason was in the stage.

The other four men had dismounted and stood staring at him. Larry Engel said impatiently: "Well, Killion, can't you get that damned woman out of your mind? We've got more important things to do than go chasing after a skirt."

Slowly Killion turned his head to look at Engel. He hated him almost as much as he hated Al Ash and Ollie Dutton, hated him so much that he told himself one of them would not be riding out of the cañon after the money was divided.

"Engel, you leave Dutton to me," Killion said in a low tone. "Him and the woman are none of your concern, but they sure are mine. They'll be staying at Finley's tonight. With a little help from Ed Horn, I'll pay a few debts back before sunup."

"Come on, come on," Chino Lopez said harshly. "You gonna sit there till you get blisters on your saddle? I want to see what my share of the *dinero* looks like."

Killion took his time dismounting. He stepped away from his horse, opened Dutton's leather bag, and dumped the contents on the grass. He froze, his eyes on one bundle of money. The greenback on top was a $1.00 bill, not $100.

Only then did Killion remember that he had not turned any of the bundles over. He had seen $100 bills, and, with his thoughts on Jean the way they had been, he had assumed that the bundles would be made up of bills of the same denomination.

The five men stood motionlessly for several

seconds, the same thought in their minds. Killion had been fooled.

Engel cursed, then shouted: "You idiot! Can't you do anything right? You saw the bills Dutton put on top and you never looked at anything else."

Engel dropped to his knees and turned the bundles over. He picked them up and quickly riffled through one end of each, then threw them back on the grass. He got to his feet, his face contorted by rage.

"We get a deal from this Bellew *hombre* who's a friend of yours," Engel said, using his tongue as if it were a whiplash. "We take ten thousand dollars from Dutton so he loses his mine, then we show up in Durango and we get another ten thousand. Four thousand apiece, which isn't much of a deal, but it's worth trying for. We stop the stage which same has a treasure box, but we let it alone. Sure, it might have had a million dollars in it, only we don't touch it because we don't want the stage company putting a gang of detectives on our tail. We don't see what the passengers have to contribute, either. We pull out with a stinking five hundred for our trouble. One hundred apiece. Chicken feed. I'm wondering if you sold out to Dutton."

Engel had been building up a towering rage. Killion watched him, knowing exactly what the man was doing. This was as good a time as any to open the ball, Killion thought, so he waited, his right hand close to the butt of his gun. Lopez stood on one side, Rafferty and Armand on the other. Still Killion wasn't sure of Lopez, but he could not risk taking his eyes off Engel.

Now Engel took a long breath, and he said in his cutting voice: "You are a jackass, Killion, a pea-brained jackass. You aren't fit to run this outfit."

That was it and Killion didn't wait. His right hand drove for his gun; he gripped the walnut butt and swept the revolver from the holster. Engel had not expected him to make his move yet, so surprise may have slowed him.

Killion's gun was level while Engel was still frantically bringing his up. Killion pulled the trigger; he felt the hard buck of the gun against his palm. He heard the roar of the shot and its echoes as they were thrown back at him, and through the cloud of smoke he saw Engel go down.

Lopez! Killion never knew what the man would do. He swung his gun in Lopez's direction, but it was instantly apparent he had no intention of buying into the fight. He stood, staring at Engel, his mouth springing open.

"How about it, Chino?" Killion asked.

Lopez whipped his head around and saw that Killion was pointing his gun at him. He backed off and threw out his hands as he yelled in a scared tone: "I'm not picking up Engel's fight, Bronc. Honest, I'm not."

Killion wheeled to face the other two. "Pig-Nose? Shorty?"

This, too, was a familiar scene to the old outlaws. Two men fighting for leadership. Or for a greater share of the loot. Or just plain cussedness. It made no difference. The challenger was dead. The leader was still the leader.

"I've got no kick," Rafferty said. "You had to do it."

Armand nodded. "He wanted to run the outfit, Bronc."

Killion holstered his gun and walked toward the dead man. He lay in the edge of the shadow thrown by a big cottonwood that grew near the stream, his outflung right hand empty, his gun a few inches away in the grass. Blood was seeping across Engel's shirt. Killion thought briefly it was too bad Larry Engel had forced the fight. They might have got along.

Now there were only four instead of five, and there would be nobody to keep an eye on Lopez the next time the blue chip was down.

Killion wheeled and, returning to where he had dropped the money, stopped and picked up the bundles of greenbacks. He tossed one to Lopez, another to Rafferty, a third to Armand, and slipped the rest into his coat pocket.

"I was all the things Engel called me," Killion said. "I guess I can't argue with any of you on that basis. You see, I knew Dutton pretty well and

I never figured he could think up a trick. He just isn't built that way, so that was how he fooled me."

Killion strode to Engel's horse. He had thought about leading the animal in case Ed Horn decided to ride with them, but that would only hold them up if they had to move fast. If Horn needed a horse, they'd have to take one of Pa Finley's. He stripped the saddle from the animal, took off the bridle, and gave him a whack on the rump. The horse trotted downstream.

Killion walked to his horse and mounted. The others stood watching him uneasily. Armand said: "Shouldn't we try to bury his carcass?"

"With our hands?" Killion asked, and shook his head. "The coyotes will take care of him."

He waited until Armand and Rafferty mounted. The three of them watched Lopez walk to the body and go through his pants pockets, dropping the money he found into his own pocket. He picked up Engel's gun and slipped it under his waistband.

Turning, Lopez saw that the others were watching him. He nodded at Killion. "No use leaving his money and gun for the Paiutes, *señor.*"

"Mount up," Killion said impatiently. He glanced at the sun, then he said: "They'll stay the night at Finley's. Horn's there. I figure we'll camp on the other side and I'll go there after dark and signal to Horn. Dutton's got that *dinero* on him or it's on the stage. I'm guessing Horn knows by this time. We'll decide how to play it after I find out from Horn where it is. If it's on Dutton, we'll know what to do when they stop the stage the next time."

Lopez leaned forward in his saddle. "*Amigo*, the *dinero* might have been in the shoe box you had."

The idea startled Killion, then he shook his head. "No, it had sandwiches in it. There was another napkin and more sandwiches below that, but she might have been carrying the money on her someway, maybe pinned inside her dress or petticoat or some damned place. Could be we'll have to undress her to find it."

He turned his horse up the slope toward the road, taking a twisting path through the quaking asps. He had made up his mind about two things he would do. He was going to kill Al Ash and he was going to take Jean with him.

VIII

The ride down the western side of the Continental Divide was a nightmare to anyone who had never made the trip before, and this was Sally Norton's first trip. In many places the road was barely wide enough to accommodate the four wheels of the coach.

Once they were over the top and headed downhill, McCoy let the big coach roll. It whipped around one curve after another at a dizzy speed. Sally sat on the outside, staring over the edge into hundreds of feet of nothing. Far below in the bottom of the cañon she could see the tips of the tall spruce trees, waiting, she thought, to receive her if the coach went over the side.

Sally shrank back against Jean who put an arm around her as she said: "Mike McCoy is a good driver, Sally. He'll get us down safely."

Johnny Roan watched Sally with honest concern. Ollie was so wrapped up in his own problem that he did not notice the girl's fear. Only Jean understood and kept her arm around Sally until the coach rounded a final sweeping curve. From here to the river the grade was not as steep as it had been higher on the mountain. A moment later they could see the bright green valley of the San Juan.

"We're almost there," Jean said as she withdrew her arm.

Sally looked at her gratefully and murmured: "Thank you. Once I get to Durango, I'll live there forever. I'll never go over this road again."

Jean shook her head. "You'll get over that after you've been here a while. I felt the same way the first time I took the stage to Durango. I've never understood how the miners get supplies to some of their mines, or how the big freight outfits are able to go over roads like this one."

"McCoy told me one time he had a dog on a rope following the stage," Johnny Roan said with a perfectly straight face, "and the dog got caught in a cramp coming around one of them curves back there."

Sally relaxed and, for the first time, smiled at him. She said: "Thanks, Johnny. I'll be all right now."

They rounded the last curve and hit the valley floor and headed straight into the setting sun, the road now almost level. The smell of dust and mountain sage was strong in the air; the leather braces grunted and groaned as the coach swept through a thick growth of quaking asps. Then the sprawling shape of the Finley house appeared ahead of them, close to the south bank of the river.

McCoy turned off the road and stopped in front of the house. He swung down, calling: "Finley place! Night stop." He walked away as two men came from the barn to unhook the horses.

Ollie opened the doors and stepped out, then helped the women down. Sally's cheeks were pale and he supported her until the ground quit lifting and dropping in waves in front of her. She was still faint even after Ollie let go.

"I'm fine now," Sally said. "You're going to spoil me."

Ollie grinned as he handed the women's valises to Johnny Roan. "Go on in," he said to Jean. "I want to talk to Pa Finley."

Roan carried the valises into the house, the two women walking beside him, Jean holding the shoe box in one hand. Horn had disappeared, but Ash and Conner remained at the coach. Finley came on toward the stage.

Finley was a big man with white hair that fell to his shoulders, a white moustache, and a long white beard. He expected people to consider him old and wise, and to regard him with reverence because he pretended to be a patriarch of sorts.

Ollie knew him too well to regard him with anything but contempt. Ollie was quite aware that he was not old, that he was almost stupid, and certainly bone lazy, demanding far more work from his hired men and his four daughters than he had any right to expect.

"Howdy, men," Finley said as he came up. "Welcome. Supper will be on the table in half an hour. I'm sorry that we're short of rooms tonight. A party of eight miners rode in early this afternoon and took four rooms. But two are still available. I just told the women passengers they could take one."

"McCoy and me will take the other one," Ash said. "We've got a heavy treasure box that we've got to watch and I don't aim to sit up all night in your bar or dining room doing it."

"All right," Finley said. "The other men will have to sleep in the barn."

"Give me a hand, Conner," Ash said. "Let's get

the box into the house. I don't know what the hell's in it, but it's heavy enough."

Ollie waited until Ash and Conner were halfway to the house, then he said: "Finley, it's time you knew. We were held up just this side of Abel Rome's place. Five men done it. The leader was Bronc Killion. I reckon you know him."

"Yeah, I do," Finley said. "How'd you recognize them? Didn't they wear masks or anything?"

"They wore bandannas," Ollie answered, "but Killion did the talking and he couldn't disguise his voice. They thought they got away with the money I was bringing from Denver. I guess you know about that. Everybody seems to have heard the story." Ollie judged that Finley wasn't above stealing the money himself if he thought he could do it. But he said: "I've still got the money, so I'm guessing they'll try again. Are you putting guards out tonight?"

"I hadn't figured on it," Finley said, his eyes still narrowed as temptation crowded him.

"I'll kill the next man who tries to take my money," Ollie said. "If you've heard the story, you know that the stakes are big."

"Sure, sure," Finley said hastily, as if not wanting Ollie to suspect that his thoughts had been about larceny. "That's what I heard. I wouldn't blame you."

"I want to know about the guards," Ollie pressed. "I hear there's a band of renegade Paiutes

144

operating around here. Now, if you aren't putting a guard out, I'll talk to McCoy."

"Paiutes?" Finley swiped a hand over his carefully brushed hair. "Well, now, I don't think no Injuns . . ."

"Damn it, are you putting a guard out or aren't you?" Ollie demanded. "Don't start lying about the Paiutes. They're in the country and you know it."

"Well, I did see some smoke to the south late this afternoon," Finley admitted. "Yeah, I'll have my men take shifts tonight."

"All right," Ollie said, and walked toward McCoy. They washed up at the horse trough together, and Ollie said: "That damned Finley had a mean thought in his head about stealing my *dinero* himself, but I think I helped him overcome temptation."

McCoy grinned. "I don't know why the company puts up with that bastard except that his girls sure can cook."

"What I'm wondering is whether we can trust his men," Ollie said. "He promised to put 'em out as guards, but the way he works 'em, they won't cotton to the notion of losing a night's sleep. By this time Killion knows he didn't get the money, so he'll be back. Finley admitted he's seen some smoke to the south. That means the Paiutes aren't far off. I'd feel safer if I knew somebody was awake around here."

"So would I," McCoy agreed.

McCoy rolled a cigarette and fired it as Johnny Roan and Conner came over and sloshed water on their faces. Then he said: "You boys want to split the night standing guard for ten dollars apiece?"

"I can use the money," Conner said. "I'll do it. We've got to sleep in the barn anyway, which same means we won't do much sleeping."

Johnny Roan's gaze whipped from Ollie to McCoy and back to Ollie. Finally he said: "I suppose that damned lieutenant has got Sally roped and tied, but I'm gonna keep trying. Even if I didn't aim to, I'd still be worried about her and Jean. That bunch of miners in the bar are a bad bunch."

"Eight of 'em," Conner said. "If they get drunk enough, they'll be hard to handle. They look mean."

"Looks like I'd better sit up in the hall outside the girls' room," Ollie said. "I'd been thinking about doing that anyhow."

"That's what I wanted to hear," Johnny said. "If you're going to do that, I'll take one shift outside. If you get into trouble in the house, just holler."

"Which do you want to take, Conner?" McCoy asked.

"The first one," Conner said.

Johnny Roan nodded. "Wake me at midnight. I'll take the rest of the night."

"OK," McCoy said. "We'll be rolling 'bout five,

which means we'll have breakfast 'bout four."

Johnny and Conner walked to the house. McCoy finished his smoke, his gaze on the coach. Ollie prowled around aimlessly, the thought in his mind that the eight miners could be Billy Bellew's men.

McCoy flipped his cigarette stub into the dust. He said: "Getting cold now that the sun's down. Let's go in and put the feedbag on. Ollie, if any man had told me a day or so ago or even this morning that I'd be paying good money to a no-good like Ted Conner and a suspected outlaw like Johnny Roan to stand guard, I'd have said he was out of his mind."

"Either one's a better investment than Ed Horn," Ollie said.

McCoy chuckled. "You're right as rain. We'd better watch Horn with both eyes. If he and Killion don't see each other before morning, I'll be surprised."

Ollie nodded. It was hard to know for sure about any man, but it seemed to him that they had to bet on Johnny Roan and Ted Conner.

IX

The instant Ollie and McCoy stepped into the house, the tantalizing aroma of cooked food came to them. Ollie looked at McCoy and swallowed. He said: "Damned if that isn't enough to make a man's mouth water."

147

"Sure is," McCoy agreed. "Fact is, my mouth is watering."

Finley was behind the bar in a room to the left. He saw Ollie and McCoy and called: "Be about five minutes till supper's on the table! Come in and have a snort."

"He don't miss a bet," Ollie muttered in disgust.

He turned into the barroom and bought a cigar that he slipped into his coat pocket. McCoy asked for a drink. Ash, Roan, and Conner were bellied up against the bar with drinks in their hands. On beyond them at the other end of the bar were the miners.

Now that Ollie had a chance to look at the miners, he agreed they were a tough-looking bunch. Seven of them wore slouch hats, dirty clothes, cowhide boots, and were bearded. The other one was smooth-shaven and clean, but his clothes were those of a miner. He looked vaguely familiar, but Ollie couldn't place him, then decided he had probably seen the man on the street in Durango or Silverton or some other nearby camp.

The smooth-shaven man strode toward Ollie and held out his hand. "I don't suppose you remember me, Dutton. I'm Monte Matt. I met you in Durango last winter. I was working a claim up the river, but the snow drove me into town."

Ollie shook hands, still having no memory of meeting the fellow, but that didn't mean anything.

There was always a fair-size floating population in a town like Durango, and he often exchanged a few words with men like this Monte Matt, either at the bar in one of the saloons or during a poker game, and then very likely never saw them again, particularly if the weather broke and they were able to get back to their mines.

"How are you, Matt?" Ollie said, seeing no purpose in telling the man he didn't remember him.

"Well, sir," Matt said in a hearty tone, "I'm in tip-top shape. When we were visiting there at the bar in the Palace, I was telling you that I had a good claim up the river and all I needed was money to develop it. Of course I couldn't do much by myself, so I've been out raising money and hiring some good men. I'm confident that before snow flies, we'll uncover the biggest vein ever found in the San Juan."

Ollie was reasonably sure now that he had never seen Matt before in his life. The Palace catered to the carriage trade and he had not been in the place more than three times. He said brusquely—"Good luck."—and turned to McCoy who was listening with wry amusement.

"Oh, Dutton, I heard about your deal with the Syndicate for the Katydid," Matt said. "I'm glad you raised the money. I've got no time for men like Billy Bellew who use the Syndicate to beat us little fellows into the ground. I hope you and your partners make a million dollars."

Ollie took a good, long look at Matt then, still not sure about him. Certainly there was nothing unusual about the man. Blue eyes, a saber-sharp nose, meaty lips, and a breath that reeked of whiskey. But again, he might have been hired by Bellew just as Bronc Killion and Ed Horn certainly had.

"Thanks," Ollie said, realizing that he had nothing except suspicions to go on, and, with circumstances the way they were, he was bound to be suspicious of all strangers.

One of the Finley girls called: "Supper's on the table!"

The miners, with Monte Matt in the lead, started in a wild rush toward the dining room. Ed Horn had just come in, and Ollie and McCoy were a few feet behind the miners, McCoy saying out of the side of his mouth: "How do you figure him?"

As Ollie stepped from the barroom into the hall that led to the stairs and separated the barroom and dining room, he realized that the miners had stopped and were staring at the stairs. Ollie turned and saw Jean and Sally Norton coming downstairs. They were rested and had changed from their traveling clothes to pretty dresses and had put up their hair. It occurred to Ollie that they were unusually attractive, but they would have been smarter to have made themselves as homely as they could.

Monte Matt's eyes actually bugged from his

head and his mouth was open as he stared at the girls.

Ollie said: "The small blonde one in the blue dress is my fiancée, Matt. We're getting married as soon as we get to Durango. The other one is engaged to a lieutenant who is stationed at Fort Lewis."

"You're lucky," Matt said. "Very lucky."

The miners went on into the dining room. Ollie turned to the stairs and, seeing that Johnny Roan had paused behind him, jerked his head at Roan to come on up. "For tonight, Sally, just pretend that Johnny is your beau. Jean, let them see your ring if you can manage it."

The girls looked at him questioningly. Jean took his arm, asking softly: "What's back of that advice?"

"Eight woman-hungry miners," Ollie said. "I wish you'd made yourselves ugly instead of pretty."

"They couldn't do that," Johnny Roan said. "Not these girls."

"Well, they could have tried," Ollie said. "Is there a lock on your door?"

"No," Jean answered. "I looked because I wanted to lock the room. I left my lunch up there, but I guess nobody will steal it during supper."

There were four places left at the end of the long table, two on each side. Ed Horn had taken the seat at the end. When Ollie and Jean sat down on one side with Sally and Roan opposite them, Horn said: "You folks are slow getting to the trough. You're taking a chance waiting to eat with this crowd at the table."

"We're not very hungry," Jean said.

Always before when Ollie had been here for a meal, he had seen Finley's four daughters. Now he watched the girls as they moved back and forth between the dining room and the kitchen, and he saw there were only three. The youngest girl, Ida, who was the only pretty one in the family, did not make an appearance.

The food was excellent as it always was: venison steaks, potatoes, beans, biscuits, honey, and gravy. The girls kept plenty of everything on the table, Norma making the rounds with a coffee pot every two or three minutes. Later Martha brought a three-layer chocolate cake into the dining room.

There was very little conversation because everyone was intent on eating. Now that they were finished, the miners rose and returned to the bar. As Finley got up to follow them, McCoy asked: "Where's Ida?"

For a moment Finley hesitated, glancing at Norma who was going around the table with the coffee pot. He said—"She's sick in bed."—and wheeled away from the table and went on into the barroom.

McCoy waited until Norma reached him, then

he asked in a tone so low that Ollie barely heard him: "What's the matter with Ida?"

Norma hesitated, looking at the hall door as if wondering if her father were listening. Then she said: "Ida isn't well, Mike."

Norma moved on to Ollie and filled his cup, and Ollie, glancing at McCoy, remembered hearing that he was fond of Ida.

Ollie knew he was sticking his nose into business that did not concern him, but he saw an expression on McCoy's face that alarmed him. He couldn't afford to let McCoy get into trouble if he could help it, so he asked: "I'd like to know a little more about Ida. Is she real sick?"

Norma had filled his cup and now filled Jean's, then she said: "You got no concern about Ida."

"Sure I'm concerned," Ollie said.

Norma had circled the end of the table and filled Sally's cup, then she looked up. "Mister Dutton, all I've got to say is that, if you and Mike or anybody else keeps asking about her, you'll make her a damned sight sicker than she is. Now forget it."

Jean was uneasy. She whispered: "You'd better forget it. Something's wrong."

Ollie nodded. "Let's go up to your room. I want to look at the door."

When they were upstairs in the girls' room, Jean picked up the shoe box and looked at it and set it back.

"Looks as if nobody bothered my lunch," Jean said in an offhand manner. "I'm worried, I guess, after Bronc Killion messed up one of my sandwiches."

"What about Ida?" Ollie asked.

"Your guess is as good as mine," Jean answered, "but there was talk last spring that Mike was engaged to marry Ida. Naturally Pa Finley was opposed to the marriage. He doesn't want to lose any of his cheap help."

"So he's making Ida stay in her room while McCoy's here?" Sally asked.

"That's my hunch," Jean said. "I saw that Norma was trying to warn you, Ollie, but you didn't savvy."

"I guess I'd better just paddle my own canoe," Ollie said ruefully. "I didn't want us left without a driver in the morning, and from the look on Mike's face I figured he was about to tear the place up." He turned around. "Better be seeing to that door."

He swung around to the door and saw that Jean was right. No lock. Not even a turn pin.

"Which room do McCoy and Ash have?" Ollie asked.

"The end one," Jean answered. "Next to us." She motioned to the wall on the north.

"All right," Ollie said. "I'm going to sit up in the hall. After Johnny and me leave, prop your chair under the knob and don't let anyone in unless you know who it is. If I'm not around, call Ash or McCoy. Johnny is standing guard outside. I'll be in the barroom for a while, then I'll be in the hall unless Johnny needs me."

"You don't really think anyone will try to break into our room, do you?" Jean asked.

"I dunno," Ollie said, "but that bunch of miners is drinking too much. If they keep it up, anything can happen." He kissed her, and, as he turned to the door, he said—"Breakfast at four."—and left the room.

X

Ollie remained in the barroom for an hour playing cards with McCoy, Horn, and Johnny Roan. Then Roan yawned and said it was time he was going to bed. Besides, Horn had all the luck and you couldn't beat a run like that.

Ollie walked to the door with Roan. Monte Matt and his miners were drinking more than they should, and Ollie was remembering what Ted Conner had said about the miners being hard to handle if they got drunk enough. They were just about that drunk now.

When they reached the door, Ollie said: "Tell Conner to get out here in front of the house if he isn't already there."

Roan stood looking up the stairs, scowling. He muttered: "I wish we were in Durango."

"So do I," Ollie said.

"I wonder what the lieutenant's like," Johnny said. "I don't reckon he's good enough for Sally no matter what he's like."

"Are you?" Ollie asked.

Roan's gaze turned to Ollie's face. "I don't know whether you're trying to be a smart aleck or not, and I know my reputation isn't what it ought to be around Durango, but I'd like to try being good enough for her."

"I wasn't being a smart aleck," Ollie said, "but I was wondering what you'd do if you got to Durango and Sally found out that her lieutenant had married another woman or was killed or had deserted. She told Jean she hadn't heard from him for a while. Anything could have happened."

"Then I'd look after her," Roan said. "I've had my share of women, most of 'em bad, but I never seen one who hit me like Sally has." He hesitated, then asked: "If you make your deal on the Katydid, would you give me a job? I mean . . . with you knowing about the things I'm supposed to have done?"

"I sure would," Ollie said.

Roan wheeled and disappeared into the darkness. McCoy had gone upstairs to his and Al Ash's room, and Ed Horn was at the bar. Ollie went upstairs, found a chair at the far end of the hall, and carried it to the door of the girls' room. He sat down, took the cigar out of his pocket, and fired it.

He saw Horn go out through the front door. Presently the miners began stringing up the stairs in various conditions, most of them so drunk they were wobbling. Monte Matt swayed back and forth and Ollie, watching, thought he was going to fall on his face before he reached his room. But he didn't, although, as he passed Ollie, his eyes were glassy and Ollie knew the miner did not recognize him.

The house became quiet, with now and then a *groan* or a *squeak* when a gust of wind hit it. Ollie heard an occasional sound that might have been a mouse gnawing on a board somewhere downstairs.

Ollie finished his cigar and rubbed out the butt. He canted his chair back against the wall and dropped off to sleep, then woke with a start when someone called: "Dutton!" He walked to the head of the stairs and saw Ted Conner standing at the foot, Ash's Winchester in his hands. He motioned for Ollie to come down.

For a moment Ollie hesitated, thinking that he shouldn't go off and leave the girls' door unguarded. Still, there was something in Conner's face that told him this was important, so he went down the stairs, saying—"I can't be gone long."—as he reached Conner.

"Come outside for a minute," Conner said.

Conner didn't wait to see if Ollie would come. He turned and walked out. Ollie hesitated, then followed, thinking that the girls would scream if anything happened. Besides, McCoy and Ash were in the next room.

Conner kept moving until he was out of the finger of lamplight that fell through the front door. He stopped and said—"Listen."—Ollie stopped, but he heard nothing except frogs *croaking* along the river and an owl *hooting* down-stream.

"I don't hear nothing unusual," Ollie said. "What's worrying you?"

"That owl," Conner said. "I never heard an owl just like that one."

"You're jumpy," Ollie said. "You can always hear an owl after dark."

Then he caught what Conner had. The owl hoot wasn't quite right, although he couldn't put his finger on what was wrong. It was just that some man had learned to make the hoot, but he needed a little more practice.

"I get it, now," Ollie said, "and I don't think it's an Indian."

"Yeah," Conner said. "That's what I thought. An Indian would do a better job than that."

"There's just one other good guess," Ollie said. "That's Bronc Killion."

"Who would he be trying to signal?" Conner demanded. "You aren't trying to tell me that he's got one of his men with us? Or with the miners?"

Ollie hesitated, remembered that Conner

wouldn't know about Ed Horn, but he might as well be told. Ted Conner and Johnny Roan weren't the kind of men to depend on, but he and McCoy were doing it tonight, so he'd better go the limit.

"Don't talk about it on the stage tomorrow to anybody," Ollie said. "We don't want to start something and we might be wrong, but Horn is a Bellew man, so he's probably the one Killion is trying to get out here for a talk."

"He admitted he was a Bellew man," Conner said, "but that don't mean he's got anything to do with Killion."

"That's the part we aren't dead sure about," Ollie agreed, "and we don't want to push him into Killion's arms if he isn't already there. Maybe he was telling the truth on the stage, but McCoy saw him and Killion together in Alamosa, so we don't trust him."

"You might be right," Conner grumbled, "but I hate to think that of Horn."

"You'd better tell Johnny when you wake him up to take his turn," Ollie said. "I guess I should have warned both of you. I don't think it makes much difference whether Killion and Horn talk or not, so don't try to stop them. Tell Johnny that, too."

Ollie turned toward the house, then paused as Conner said: "Dutton, you need help and you're going to need it till you get to Durango and lay that *dinero* down in front of Billy Bellew. I figure you've still got it."

"That's right," Ollie said. "I've still got it."

"Well, I don't stack up very high around Durango," Conner said. "Raising pigs isn't the kind o' work that makes folks cotton to you. Then I got my wife out of a house and that shuts her off from having any friends among the decent women in Durango. What I'm trying to say is that I've got to do something different. I've got a few relatives living around Denver and I went out there hoping they'd grubstake me so I could go prospecting. I sold my pigs before I left Durango. My wife's living alone till I get back. I didn't raise any money. Now I've got to have a job. After you get the Katydid, you think you'd give me one?"

"Sure," Ollie said. "If we get to Durango in time and we're still alive."

"I know," Conner said gloomily. "It's a good bet that we aren't all gonna be alive when the stage pulls into Durango."

As Ollie turned back to the house, he thought about Johnny Roan who had asked the same question earlier in the evening. Johnny hoped to make himself worthy of Sally Norton if she didn't marry her lieutenant, and Ted Conner had sold his pig business, hoping he could hold his wife who had been a prostitute.

The odds against both men were long, and Ollie

found himself admiring them. At least they were trying to make respectable lives for themselves. On the other hand, Bronc Killion had been respectable and he had chosen to go the wrong way. It was Ollie's guess that Ed Horn was taking the same route Killion had.

As Ollie reached the hall, he had a fleeting glimpse of someone just disappearing above him at the head of the stairs. He took three steps at a time, and, when he reached the upstairs hall, he saw a woman at the far end. She was standing there, looking uncertainly at one door and then another.

Ollie strode silently toward her and said: "Ida."

She whirled to face him, a hand flying to her mouth to shut off an involuntary sound.

"Mister Dutton," she said in a low voice. "I didn't know you were awake. I thought everybody was asleep."

"All but me," he said. "I understood that you were sick in bed."

She stepped toward him, turning her face so that her right cheek was in the light from the bracket lamp above Ollie. He saw the purple bruise and guessed what had happened. He asked: "Your dad?"

"That's right, Mister Dutton," she said. "I've got marks on my back, too. He used a whip on me. I told him this morning that I was going away with Mike McCoy. We've been engaged for months, but I wasn't eighteen until yesterday. Pa can't legally make me stay here, but I'm slave labor like my sisters, and he won't let me go."

"I'll tell Mike," Ollie said, "and he'll go to the sheriff. Your dad ought to be in jail."

"That's where he belongs," she said, "but I can't wait. He'll kill me if he has to. He's a mean man, Mister Dutton. Meaner than you could even guess. I've got to go away with Mike tomorrow. I can't stay here."

So there will be trouble after all, Ollie thought. He scratched his head and looked at Ida and didn't know what to say or do.

Ida gripped his arms. "Mister Dutton, I've got to see Mike right now. I've got to talk to him. Which room does he have?"

Ollie looked at the bruise on her cheek and he sensed the paralyzing fear that was in her. He sighed, realizing he was sticking his nose into this problem that still was none of his business. He said: "It's the room on the end. I'll go in and wake Mike. You stay here till I get you."

As he gripped the doorknob and slowly turned it, he told himself that Ida did not realize the trouble she would have been in if she had made the wrong guess and had gone into one of the miner's rooms instead of McCoy's.

XI

The sun was down by the time Killion turned off the road to the river, a half mile beyond Finley's buildings. He glanced around, noting the good grass of the meadow, and nodded. "This will do," he said, dismounting. "Chino, take care of the horses. I'll rustle some wood."

Armand and Rafferty always did the cooking. In the past Lopez and Engel had divided the chore of taking care of the horses. Now that Engel was gone, Lopez shrugged and accepted all of the job of horse tending. Killion picked up several armloads of dry driftwood that had been carried downstream by the last spring run-off and dropped them beside the fire Armand had started.

"Keep the fire small," Killion said. "We aren't very far from Finley's. The chances are he's got guards out, with all this talk about the renegade Indian band. We don't want Finley to see our fire and come down to investigate."

Armand nodded and said nothing. When Killion had brought as much wood as he thought they would use, he sat down on a drift log at the edge of the water and rolled and fired a cigarette. Presently Lopez came to the fire and hunkered down a few feet from him.

Darkness had come with only the starlight and the red glow of the campfire to break it. Presently

Rafferty called: "Come and get it before I throw it out!"

Killion had a strange feeling as he ate. Perhaps it was the kind of feeling he should expect after killing Larry Engel, although he had killed men before and had never had a feeling quite like this. It seemed to him he had reached the end of one period of his life when he had left Durango with his two friends and held up the stage. He had been wounded and his friends killed, and thus had been started on a career.

Well, he wouldn't be rich when he finished this job, but he'd have enough to get out of the country and make a new start somewhere else. One thing he had learned after that first abortive hold-up. If a man followed the Owlhoot long enough, he'll come to a violent end, either with a bullet in his brisket as Larry Engel had done, or he'd be dancing on air and looking at the sky. If a man had any sense, he'd quit before either happened.

The part of the future he was uncertain about was what to do with Jean Mason. He could, as he had once decided, take her with him after they stopped the stage, but he knew it wouldn't be smart. She would slow him up, and, if there was any crime that would make the country buzz like a hive of angry bees, it was kidnapping a woman.

He had considered another alternative, that of visiting Jean after she arrived in Durango. That was a smarter thing to do; he had to go back to

Durango anyway to collect from Billy Bellew. As soon as he had his money and when he was finished with Jean, he'd get across the state line into New Mexico Territory and keep going. He was certain that he would finish with Jean. She was a fever in his blood that had to be satisfied.

He was going to bring an end to Al Ash's career, too, when they stopped the stage. That was another piece of unfinished business he had to take care of. If he rubbed Ollie Dutton out when he was in Durango, that would be ending this chapter with just the right touch.

He finished his second cup of coffee. As he put the tin cup down and reached for the makings, Shorty Armand said: "We figure we'd better tell you, Bronc. This is our last job. We've been riding the Owlhoot a long time. We've got some money in a Pueblo bank, and, with what we get out of this job, we'll get along."

Killion knew what they were thinking. They hadn't liked his shooting Larry Engel. They'd said he had to do it and all that, which meant they weren't going to buck him.

He saw no reason to tell them he was calling it quits, too. He only nodded and said: "I don't blame you."

Rafferty had been watching him to see if he was going to do anything about it. Now Killion sensed that both men were relieved. Rafferty said: "We'll ride south to Las Cruces or maybe go on over to Tucson and sit in the sun the rest of our lives. We might even wind up being good, honest citizens."

Lopez snickered. "The hell you will. You'll settle down about a month, and then you'll see a bank that looks easy and you'll take a whack at it."

"No, we won't," Armand said. "All we want is to see the end of this job. Then we're quitting."

Killion smoked his cigarette, thinking that Lopez was right. Men like Armand and Rafferty had followed their trade too long. They weren't destined to end their lives sitting in the sun and dying with their boots off, but that was their business and none of his, so he let them live with their illusion.

He brought his saddle and blanket to the fire and made up his bed. He'd wait a while before trying to talk to Ed Horn, so he lay down, his head on the saddle, and stared at the sky through the limbs of a quaking asp.

The thought came to Killion that maybe he was like Armand and Rafferty, that once a man starts riding the Owlhoot, he's never able to make the break, that this chapter was the last and would end in violence just as it would for the two old outlaws. A chill traveled down his spine. He had a hunch he had overplayed his hand, too.

Killion woke, startled to realize that he had dropped off to sleep in spite of his intention to stay awake, that it was getting along toward midnight and it was time to move. He rose and slipped away into the darkness, saying nothing to Lopez or the others who were asleep.

When he reached the clearing that held the Finley buildings, he crouched in the willows by the river and hooted like an owl. He saw a man go into the house and come back with another man; Dutton, Killion guessed as he appeared briefly in the lamplight. A minute or so after that Dutton went back. A few seconds later he heard Horn's low voice: "Killion?"

"Here," Killion said, and Horn materialized out of the darkness.

"I thought it was about time for you to show up," Horn said. "What did you find in Dutton's leather bag?"

"Money," Killion answered.

"How much?"

"About six hundred dollars. He had one-hundred dollar bills on top, but the rest of each package was one-dollar bills. I should have taken a closer look, but I knew Dutton pretty well. He's not a tricky man."

"No," Horn said, "but even a man like Dutton gets tricky when he's got a big enough stake to play for. I guess you weren't very smart."

"I guess not," Killion said, more irritated than he wanted Horn to know. "Larry Engel said that when we took a look at the money. He's dead now. He was a little slow on the draw."

Horn was silent for a time and Killion hoped he got the point. Killion had been stupid; he had admitted it, and he wanted that to be the end of it.

Finally Horn said: "I'm not looking for a shooting match with you, but I want you to keep your end of the bargain."

"Do you know where the money is?" Killion asked.

"No, though I've bumped up against Dutton enough to be fairly sure he's not wearing a heavy money belt. I've noticed that the girl hangs onto the lunch box you looked into. Of course, that might be another trick. She could have it on her. Maybe each bill is pinned to her clothes."

"Got any ideas about how I should work it?" Killion asked.

"Just one," Horn answered. "I don't cotton to the idea of stopping the stage again and having everybody get off like you did before. You're one man short, now that Engel's not with you. Another thing is you've got to keep looking till you find it and that could be a little hard out there in the open on the road. You might have to undress the girl, and that would make Dutton and the rest do things they wouldn't do otherwise."

"All right, let's have the idea," Killion said.

"Why not move into the Bear Creek station? That's a dinner stop, not a night stop, and it doesn't have many men. Just one couple who do the cooking and one stock tender. You can take care of them without any trouble and be ready for the stage, which gets in early in the afternoon, close to one, I think."

Killion thought about it for a minute, then he said: "You going to give me a hand this time?"

"Not unless I have to," Horn said. "I don't want to come out into the open if I can help it, so I'd rather have you handle it."

"All right," Killion said, "we'll be there."

"Keep your eyes open for that Paiute band," Horn warned. "Your scalps are just as good to them as if you were honest citizens."

"We'll watch it," Killion said stiffly. "So long."

He slipped away and returned to camp. When he got there, he saw that Lopez was brooding at the fire. Killion wondered about that, then he shrugged. When this was over, he would probably have to kill Lopez or be killed. Lopez had liked Larry Engel too well to let it go.

Killion tried to sleep, but could not. Jean Mason was back in his thoughts again. It might work out for him at the Bear Creek station. It would sure be safer than trying to find her in Durango.

XII

Ollie slipped into McCoy's and Ash's bedroom and closed the door. He called: "Mike!"

For a moment there was no answer, then he heard Al Ash's cold voice. "Who is it? I've got my gun in my hand. If you're after the treasure box, you'll get your head blowed off."

"It's Ollie. You fellows act like you never heard my voice before," he said.

"Strike a match and light the candle on the bureau," Ash said. "If you're anybody but Ollie Dutton, you're dead."

"I don't want to be dead," Ollie said in disgust, "so get a good look before you pull the trigger. It will be a fine spring day in hell before I try doing Mike a favor again."

Ollie struck a match and held it to his face, then lighted the candle on the bureau. Ash said: "You look a little bit like Ollie Dutton, all right."

"You can't blame us, Ollie," McCoy said, "waking us up in the middle of the night. You might have been one of the miners or one of Killion's outfit. Or even Pa Finley himself. I sure don't trust that booger."

Ollie said: "You've got a lady waiting in the hall to see you. When you talk to her, you'll think less of Pa Finley than you do now."

"Wait a minute," Ash said. "I'm not entertaining no woman in a bedroom this time of night. I got nothing on but my drawers. Damn it, keep her out . . ."

McCoy didn't listen. He opened the door and Ida slipped into the room, and for the next few seconds neither was aware of anyone else in the whole world. For a moment they stood looking at each other, then McCoy opened his arms and Ida threw her arms around him. As they hugged and kissed each other, Ash put his revolver down and jumped back into bed and pulled a blanket over him.

"By grab," Ash muttered, "it's getting so a man can't even sleep without a woman coming in and hugging and kissing the stage driver."

Ida drew away from McCoy and looked over his shoulder. "Are you telling me that everywhere you two go, women come into your bedroom and hug and kiss this stage driver?"

"You're lying to her," McCoy said angrily. "Now straighten this out or I'll cut your throat."

Ash rubbed his face with both hands and shook his head. Finally he said: "Well, Ida, I'd like to worry both of you, but you heard what that desperado you've been kissing just said. He'll cut my throat if I don't straighten this out, so to save my life I have to tell you I spoke with a forked tongue. It is true I have seen a woman come into our bedroom where she had no business in the first place and hug and kiss this stage driver, but since I am an honest man wishing to keep my throat from being cut, I will admit it was you."

"I think you're both a pair of liars," Ida said. "Mister Dutton, what do you think?"

Ollie knew he should be back in the hall, but he was still laughing. Al Ash, sitting up in bed with a blanket pulled under his chin, was about the funniest sight he had seen for a long time.

"Oh, I expect they're both liars," Ollie said, "but for once, Al is probably telling the truth. Of course, he is a blood-thirsty booger who wanted to shoot me a little while ago, but . . ."

Ollie heard something in the hall and stopped, his head cocked. It was a banging noise, but it didn't mean anything until the girls in the next room screamed. He wheeled and plunged into the hall, realizing that the noise he had heard was someone trying to break into the girls' room.

The instant he was through the door of Ash's and McCoy's bedroom, he saw Monte Matt in front of Jean's and Sally's room. Apparently Jean had blocked their door with a chair as Ollie had told her to do, and now Matt had stepped back and was about to smash it open with his shoulder.

Matt never reached the door. Ollie got to him first, his temper boiling over into a murderous fury. He hit Matt on the jaw, a sledge-hammer blow that knocked the miner flat on his back at the head of the stairs.

"Get up," Ollie said. "Get up so I can beat you to death."

Matt sat up and shook his head. He was still too drunk to know what he was doing, but Ollie's blow had cleared some of the cobwebs out of his brain. The doors to the miners' rooms were flung open, then McCoy called from the end of the hall: "Stand pat! I'll shoot any of you who jump into this fracas. Matt deserves anything he gets."

The miners stood motionlessly in front of their doors as Matt looked up at Ollie. He whimpered: "Don't hit me any more."

"Get up," Ollie said. "Get up or I'll kick you to death where you are."

Matt grabbed a post at the head of the stairs and pulled himself to his feet. Ollie hit him again, a looping uppercut that caught Matt squarely on the point of the chin and snapped his head back. The blow knocked him loose from the post and sent him crashing down the stairs head over heels.

He didn't stop until he reached the hall at the foot of the stairs. There he sprawled out full length and lay motionlessly, blood trickling down his chin, arms flung out on both sides of him. Ollie, looking down at him, thought for an instant he was dead. He had the appearance of a rag doll that had been tossed to the floor by a child.

Pa Finley, wearing a long, white nightgown, ran into the hall from the dining room, a shotgun in his hands. He looked at Ollie who stood at the head of the stairs, then at the unconscious Monte Matt, and demanded: "What started this?"

"He tried to get into the girls' room," Ollie said. "If he isn't dead, he deserves to be."

Finley knelt beside Matt, laid his shotgun on the floor, and felt the man's pulse. He rose, the gun in his hand. "He's alive, all right. He was too drunk to know what he was doing. You didn't have to be this rough on him."

"You think being drunk would excuse him if he'd got that door open?" Ollie demanded. "Finley, you're the one who's really responsible. You kept on selling him drinks when you knew he'd had all he could handle."

"Send some of those men down here to carry Matt to his room," Finley said, and turned and disappeared into the dining room.

Ollie backed up to the girls' room. "Get down there and haul him back to his room," he said to two of the miners. "If he ever tries that again, I'll kill him."

"He won't," one of the miners said.

They carried him up the stairs, grunting under his weight. When they reached the upstairs hall, they set him on his feet, but he was still rubber-legged, his head lolling on his chest.

The miners drew back into their rooms and shut their doors. Ollie glanced at McCoy and nodded. "Thanks, Mike. You kept them off my back."

"One good turn deserves another," McCoy said. "Did Finley go back to bed?"

"I guess so," Ollie said. "He's not in sight."

McCoy stepped into his room. Then Ollie realized that Jean had poked her head through the door. She whispered: "Are you all right, Ollie?"

"Oh, sure," he said. "I'm sorry you were scared."

"I guess we weren't really scared," Jean said. "But where were you?"

"In McCoy's and Ash's room," Ollie said. "Ida came upstairs to see Mike, and I woke him up for her."

"She's in there now?" Jean asked.

"Yes," Ollie answered. "She said she had to see him. Go back to bed. It won't be long till they'll be hollering breakfast."

She pulled her head back and shut the door. Ollie sat down and canted his chair back against the wall. Jean hadn't said so, but it was plain enough she had not approved of Ollie's getting involved in Ida's and McCoy's problems.

Jean didn't know, of course, that, if Ollie had not been involved, McCoy would not have been in the hall and the miners would have been on Ollie's back. If that had happened, they probably would have killed him before they were done.

XIII

Ida Finley was paralyzed with fear from the instant she heard the racket in the hall. She pressed against the wall, her eyes wide, her hands clenched at her sides. When she heard her father's voice from the foot of the stairs, she began to tremble.

She was still trembling when McCoy came back into the room and shut the door. Ida whispered: "Where's Pa?"

"He went back to bed, I guess," McCoy said. "He isn't out there any more."

"Mike, Mike," Ida whispered, and ran to him and threw her arms around him. "You've got to get me out of here. I can't live this way. He'll kill me if I stay."

He held her in his arms, her face pressed against his chest until she quit trembling, then he pushed her back, asking: "Now what's this all about?"

She wiped her eyes with her handkerchief, then she walked to the bureau and, picking up the candle, held the flame to the side of her face. "See what he did to me?" she asked, and handed the candle to him. "Pull my blouse away from my neck so you can see what my back looks like."

He obeyed and began to curse when he saw the long, raw marks that ran down her back. "Why in the hell did he do it?" McCoy demanded.

"I'm eighteen now," she said. "I've worked like a slave for him for years just the way my mother did until he worked her to death and the way my sisters have, but now I want my own home and I'm going to have it. I love you, Mike. I'm not going to waste the rest of my life working for Pa. I told him this morning and I said I was going to Durango with you." She swallowed and went on. "He hit me on the side of the face with his fist, then he sent me to my room. After a while he came in with a blacksnake and whipped me on the back and said he'd kill me if I tried to leave.

He said I had to stay and work for him as long as the stage stopped here and he had a good business."

"The bastard," McCoy said in a low tone. "The dirty, stinking bastard. I'll kill him."

"What kind of a husband would you make after they hang you for murder?" Ida shook her head. "I want you alive."

"Well, you can't stay here," McCoy said. "Do you want to get on the stage in the morning and go with me? We'll get married as soon as we get to Durango."

"I want to go with you," Ida said, "but I'm not going to get on the stage here. It would just make trouble. Pa is a coward, but he knows that, if I leave, my sisters will go, too. They stay because they're afraid to leave. After the way he beat me, they're more scared than ever. He'll fight to make me stay. I've always been the rebel. The other girls are older than I am, but they've always looked at me to see what I was going to do."

McCoy sat down on the side of the bed and wiped his face. "I'll do whatever you say, Ida. I don't want to kill him. No matter how bad a man he is, it would always be between us, but I will kill him before I'll leave you here for him to murder."

"I'm not going to stay here," she said. "I'll leave tonight. He won't miss me until after you're gone in the morning. He thinks he hurt me so much I'll be in bed for several days. He might not even miss me until evening unless one of the girls tells him. He'll probably go back to bed after the stage leaves and sleep until noon."

"You can't leave here tonight," McCoy said. "It isn't safe. The Indians are too close."

"I'll be scared," she admitted, "but I'm a lot more scared to stay here. I'll meet you on the road tomorrow. I don't know how far I'll get, but it will be a mile or more down the river from here. You stop and pick me up and we'll be in Durango by night. He won't come after me that far because he's afraid he'll be arrested for beating me. I told him I'd put him in jail the rest of his life if I could."

"Ida, the Indians . . . ," McCoy began.

"They won't see me," she said, "so quit worrying about that. They haven't been seen around here. They're a long ways to the west, the last I heard. Besides, I'm no greenhorn. I can take care of myself."

McCoy got up and walked around the room. She was right. She wasn't a greenhorn; she could take care of herself, and, if she stayed here, she would be seriously injured, perhaps killed. It was unbelievable that a father would murder his daughter, but what he had already done to her was unbelievable.

"All right," he said finally. "I don't like to have you do it, but maybe it's less dangerous for you to go than to stay here. You'd better get started. Don't go any farther than you have to."

"I guess I'm throwing myself at you," she said, "and I didn't want to do that. If you'd rather wait and not get married for a while . . ."

"Don't talk that way," he said harshly. "Of course, I want to get married. Now you'd better get started."

He opened the door and looked along the hall. Ollie Dutton was catnapping in his chair. He stirred as Ida walked past him and opened his eyes, but he didn't say anything. She went on down the stairs. McCoy stood in the doorway of his bedroom, listening, but he heard nothing, so he shut the door and crossed the room to the window.

"You're a fool, Mike," Ash said hotly. "The company will fire you. Old Finley may be as mean as hell, but he runs a good place and the company likes what he does. When he goes to the company and says you helped one of his girls run away, they'll kick you all the way from Durango to Alamosa."

"Shut up," McCoy said gloomily. "I know all of that, but I can't do anything else."

He stared into the darkness, thinking he saw her move silently across the yard toward the river. One of Finley's dogs began to bark, then was silent, and McCoy guessed she had spoken to the dog. He wished that the guard knew she was leaving, but maybe she could slip past him. Then he thought of Bronc Killion and his gang and he wondered if they were somewhere around the Finley place.

He turned to the bed. "Well, Al, you say I'm a fool. What would you have done?"

"Blow out the candle," Ash said, "and come to bed. Sure you're a fool. Any time a man gets tangled up with a woman, he's a fool. Look at Johnny Roan making a fool out of himself over Sally Norton while she's going to Durango to marry a lieutenant. And I'll bet that right now Bronc Killion is thinking about Jean more'n he is the money he's trying to steal from Ollie. And Ted Conner trying to keep that woman of his who's no good and never was."

"You didn't answer my question," McCoy said.

"Well, I didn't much want to," Ash said. "If I was in your boots, I'd be just as big a fool as you are. Now will you come to bed?"

McCoy blew out the candle and lay down. He stared at the dark ceiling, thinking of her alone out there in the darkness, not knowing about Killion's outfit, or about the Indians.

When Ollie knocked on the door and told McCoy breakfast was ready, he felt completely worn out. All he could hope for was that Ida was somewhere down the river waiting for the stage and that she was safe.

XIV

No more than a hint of dawn was in the sky above the Continental Divide to the east when Ollie crossed the yard toward the barn.

Johnny Roan appeared out of the darkness, recognized Ollie, and asked: "Everything all right?"

"Sure is," Ollie answered. "Go in for breakfast. Anything happen?"

"No," Roan said, and then changed his mind. "Well, I'm not sure. When it's as dark as it's been all night, it's pretty hard to know what's going on, but I thought I seen someone sneak out of the house and disappear downstream. I kind o' figured on shooting at him, and then I decided it wasn't any of my business. Didn't seem like we had to watch anybody but Horn and he's in the barn."

Ollie thought it was possible that Ida had slipped out of the house during the night. He said: "You did the right thing. Go on in. I'll wake up the others."

Ollie walked to the barn, opened the door, and yelled that breakfast was ready. As he returned to the house, he couldn't keep from being uneasy about Ida. With the renegade Indians in the country and with Killion's outfit camped some-where around here, the girl wasn't safe out there by herself and Ollie was surprised that McCoy had let her do it this way. Still, he knew this was the only way to avoid trouble with Pa Finley.

Jean and Sally were coming down the stairs when Ollie entered the house. Jean looked tired and Sally was yawning. Ollie said: "Good morning, though neither one of you look like it's a good morning."

"Sure it's a good morning," Jean said. "It was just a short night."

Pa Finley was sitting at one end of the long table, McCoy and Ash at the other end. McCoy was dark-faced, his anger plainly close to the boiling point. He avoided looking at Finley and had already filled his plate with flapjacks, fried eggs, bacon, and had started to eat.

"We'll roll in about fifteen minutes," McCoy said curtly as he got up from the table.

McCoy left the house with Al Ash. The stock tenders were hooking up the horses to the coach. Ollie said in a low voice to Conner who sat beside him: "Were Finley's men up standing guard with you and Johnny?"

Conner shot a glance at Finley, then he said out of the corner of his mouth: "No. They told me they'd rather have their hair lifted than to work all day and stand guard all night."

Ollie nodded. It was what he had expected. Finley was notorious for not being able to keep his help. He paid top wages, but he expected two men's work out of each one, and in a country like this where mines were needing help and prospectors were making big strikes, no one worth his salt would stay very long at a road ranch unless he was broke, and then he'd be on his way as soon as he had earned a grubstake.

Ollie couldn't keep from thinking about Ida's sisters. If Ida succeeded in running away, the others would likely follow. Finley was no fool. He would know that, so he'd certainly be after Ida as soon as he found out she was gone.

The passengers were in the yard with their luggage in less than fifteen minutes, Jean holding onto the shoe box. As Ollie helped her into the coach, he wished that he had done something else with the money. If Killion's gang stopped the stage again, the shoe box would be checked more carefully than it had been yesterday. Killion would not overlook it a second time.

He knew then that he would have to fight if the stage was stopped today, although a fight would endanger Jean's and Sally's lives. But he had to measure that danger against the greater danger that Killion would kidnap Jean. When he considered that, he knew there was no choice.

He was still thinking about it when he realized that McCoy was stopping the stage. His first thought was: *This is it.* He eased his gun out of the holster, then he glanced out and saw Ida standing at the side of the road and felt foolish and relieved.

"It isn't a hold-up," Ollie said, and opened the door and stepped out as soon as the coach stopped.

"Looking for a ride, ma'am?" McCoy asked.

Ida was cold and scared and in no mood for humor.

The other men were out of the coach now, Ted Conner saying: "I'll ride on top, Mike. She'll be warmer inside."

"I guess she will," McCoy agreed. "Get in. We've got to keep rolling."

Ollie gave Ida a hand and she stepped into the stage. Then they were all in and seated and the coach was rolling again.

Ida shivered and looked at Ollie. She said: "Mister Dutton, I think it's only fair that everybody should know I'm running away and my father will come after me as soon as he finds out I'm gone. There may be trouble."

"You're of age," Ollie said. "You've got a right to go where you want to when you want to."

"If there's trouble," Horn said, "we'll take care of it for you."

Ida turned to look at him. She said: "Just so there won't be a misunderstanding. I'd also better tell you that I'm going to marry Mike McCoy."

"Congratulations," Horn said. "You're getting a good man. I respect Mike McCoy."

"We all do," Ollie said.

Johnny Roan pinned his gaze on Sally's face. "This must be a lovers' coach. Cupid is sure riding with us."

Sally didn't snap at him. She smiled and said:

"He'll ride all the way to Durango with us, Johnny. He might even go on to Fort Lewis."

"Yeah, he might," Johnny grumbled.

Ollie was nodding, the long, sleepless night beginning to catch up with him. His head tipped toward Jean's shoulder, then he woke when Ida said sharply: "Mister Dutton."

Ollie shook his head, his eyes snapping open. "Well now, you're safe and I'm glad because I was a mite worried about you, so if you'll excuse me, I'll go back to . . ."

"There's something I've got to tell you," she said impatiently. "I should have told Mike. I walked along the road after I left the house last night and kept going until I got to the meadow we just left. I almost went too far before I realized some men were camped there. I was afraid to go past them, so I hid in the brush. They got up before daylight and cooked breakfast and rode out just a little while ago."

"How many?"

"Four."

Killion had five men including himself. Ollie thought about that, then he asked: "You know any of them?"

"I knew Bronc Killion," she answered. "He's been on the stage several times and stayed overnight at Pa's place. I couldn't catch much of their talk, but I did hear Killion say they had to get somewhere before the stage did."

"You couldn't make out where they meant?" Ollie asked.

"No, that's all I heard," Ida said. "You suppose they're after the treasure box?"

"Yeah, that's probably it," Ollie said, and noted the grin on Ed Horn's lips.

Ollie settled back and closed his eyes, a feeling of hopelessness settling over him. He had guessed Killion would try again, but he had not known when or where. He still didn't. There were no great mountain ranges to cross between here and Durango, but Killion could certainly find plenty of places where the stage could be stopped and held up.

The stage wheeled on toward Durango, and Bear Creek station, but Ollie did not sleep. Every nerve was tense as he waited for what was certain to happen.

XV

At first there was no hint of a cloud anywhere, then, as the morning wore on, thunderheads began poking above the horizon to the west. They would be in a storm before the day was over, Killion thought absently, and stared ahead at the crest of the next hill.

He sensed a strange kind of wildness about this country that appealed to him. Now and then they passed a prospector's cabin and a hole he had gouged into the side of the hill and then, finding only country rock, had gone off and left it. They jumped several deer that bounded away through the timber. Once they passed a great elk in a meadow; he raised his head to look at them, then moved in his dignified way into the quaking asps.

A glance at the sun told Killion it was nearly noon, so they were not far from Bear Creek station. The hour of reckoning, then, was at hand. For some reason the wildness that he felt around him took possession of him and turned into a sullen sort of rebellion.

He was doing Billy Bellew's dirty work for him, robbery and murder, with maybe a rope for a reward in the end. And what was he getting from Bellew? A paltry $4,000 or $5,000. Maybe he'd better have a little more for his trouble. Bellew and the Syndicate were making a fortune out of a $10,000 investment, and all that they had to do was to sit on their fat behinds. No, there was no justice in that.

For some reason Killion's mind turned back to the good days when he had been Ollie Dutton's friend and had thought Jean Mason loved him. No fear then, no running, no jumping at shadows, no worrying about the law.

Killion couldn't help wondering why he didn't have enough sense to realize that there were other women in the world besides Jean, that if she wanted Ollie Dutton, she didn't want Bronc Killion. But, no, he . . .

"Bronc."

Killion pulled up and looked back at Shorty Armand who was pointing at the ground.

"What is it?" Killion asked harshly.

"Here's some tracks you'd better come and look at," Armand said. "Maybe I ain't reading 'em right."

Lopez dismounted and squatted beside the road, peering at the ground. Rafferty, still in the saddle, said: "You'll read 'em the same as we do, Bronc. There's only one way you can read 'em, and the message isn't what I like to read."

"They went by not more'n an hour ago," Lopez said, fingertips tracing the hoofprints in the soft earth. "Less, I'd say."

Swearing softly, Killion rode back and dismounted. He stiffened, his hard breathing sawing into the sudden quiet. A band of riders had crossed the road going south. The horses had not been shod, and there had been at least a dozen in the party.

Killion faced the others. "You're right," he said to Rafferty. "There's only one way to read this message. The Indian renegades we've been hearing about are heading back for the reservation."

"Maybe," Rafferty said. "Maybe not. They know as well as we do that there's some hair to be lifted at the Bear Creek station. I say there's a hell of a good chance that they're headed in that direction, once they cross the road."

Killion shook his head. "I don't think so. They wouldn't have to cross the road at all if they were going to Bear Creek."

Killion mounted and rode on, not wanting them to know that his heart was bouncing around in his chest like a rubber ball. He wasn't going to tell Rafferty, but he had a hunch the man was right, that the Paiute renegades would tackle the Bear Creek station. The road ran through open country from here to the station, so there seemed to be little chance that he and his men could be ambushed.

As he remembered the station's buildings, they were in a sizable clearing just east of Bear Creek, with a scrub oak jungle to the south. That was where the danger would be. The renegades wouldn't ride at them in a wild charge, screaming their war cries. No, they'd hide in the scrub oak and shoot the whites down without showing as much as a hair on their heads.

Killion told himself that it was enough to have to buck men like Al Ash and Mike McCoy and Ollie Dutton without worrying about a dozen dirty, skulking Paiutes who should be across the state line in Utah where they belonged. The temptation was strong to turn back, or to hold up the stage somewhere else.

Then Killion thought: *To hell with it!* He'd made

the plan with Ed Horn and he'd go ahead with it.

Half an hour later they reached the clearing that held the stage station. It was exactly as Killion remembered it, a two-room log cabin, a log barn, three small outbuildings, and several corrals. The creek ran on the other side of the cabin. The scrub oak was within rifle range to the south, but in the other directions the pine trees were so scattered that they offered no real concealment for any ambushers.

Wood smoke rose from the chimney of the cabin. A man was leading two horses to the creek to water them. Now Killion, riding slowly, his muscles tense, every nerve tight, studied the scrub oak, but he saw nothing that alarmed him. Absolutely nothing. He began to relax.

When they reached the cabin and dismounted, a second man stepped out of the cabin and called: "You men want anything?"

"Yeah, we want some dinner," Killion said. "We've come all the way from Finley's place and we're hungry."

Killion dismounted and walked toward the man who stood in the doorway. He was middle-aged, stocky of build, and wore a dirty white apron. The man who had been watering the horses came across the yard. He was old, stooped, and white-haired, with big hands and enlarged knuckles of one who has labored hard all of his life. Killion glanced at him and for a brief moment felt compassion for him. He didn't know it, but he had come to the end of his string.

The man in the doorway shook his head. "I'm sorry, boys, but I can't get dinner for you. I'm the cook and I just ain't got time. My wife usually does the cooking, but I sent her to Durango on account of the Indian scare, so me and old man Fields are the size of it. The stage is due purty quick and I've got to feed them first, but if you want to hang around and see if there's anything left after the stage leaves . . ."

He was still talking when Chino Lopez, standing ten feet behind Killion and to one side, shot him in the chest, the heavy slug knocking him back into a sprawling heap in the middle of the room. The man, caught in the yard between the house and the barn, wheeled and started to run in an awkward, frantic gait, but he couldn't outrun Lopez's second bullet that caught him in the back. He staggered and fell forward into the dust.

"Put the horses away," Killion said to Armand and Rafferty. "We don't want 'em in sight when the stage rolls in. Chino, we'll move the bodies to that shed yonder, then we'll have time to rustle some grub before our company gets here."

Lopez nodded as he holstered his gun. They picked up the man who was in the cabin as Armand and Rafferty led the four horses to the creek. Killion and Lopez dumped the body onto the floor of the shed, went back and picked up the man who was in the open, and threw him on top of the other dead man, then Killion closed the door.

Neither said a word. Lopez had shot the two men without orders. It was something Killion would have to settle later. Both men were to be killed, but it had been Killion's prerogative to say when and where and by whom. It underscored what Killion already knew—once the job was finished and the money was in their hands, Lopez would kill him or he would have to kill Lopez.

All four men were in the open when firing broke out from the scrub oak. Killion lunged toward the cabin the instant he heard the first shot. Lopez screamed and Killion was vaguely aware that the man had thrown up his hands and was staggering and falling, but he didn't look back or make any effort to help Lopez. Killion had only one objective—to get through the door into the safety of the cabin.

Armand and Rafferty whirled and started toward shelter, but they hadn't gone ten feet until they were down. Rafferty struggled to his feet, one hand clutching his abdomen, but he stumbled and fell when he was still twenty feet from the barn. This time he stayed down.

Killion had almost reached the doorway of the cabin when he felt a numbing blow hit his left shoulder. He stumbled and fell forward, not knowing how hard he had been hit, but knowing that he had to get out of the doorway to the safety of the log wall inside.

He scrambled on his hands and knees, and then rolled in a frantic effort to get clear of the doorway. Bullets flew above him and slashed into the opposite wall. Others slapped into the floor beside him. Time spun out so that these few seconds seemed to be an eternity before he rolled up against the base of the front wall. The shooting stopped almost as suddenly as it had started.

For a while he lay there, sobbing and groaning as he labored for breath, and all the time he kept wondering if the murdering devils would rush him. He felt for his revolver. It was still in the holster, but he would never be able to turn a charge of a dozen men with his six-shooter. Several minutes passed and he thought that maybe the Indians had left.

He was bleeding. He dug his bandanna out of his pants pocket and, wadding it up, slid it under his shirt and pressed it against the wound. Suddenly he remembered that the stage would be along soon and Jean Mason was on it.

He knew that it was stupid to think the renegades had pulled out. If McCoy wasn't warned, he'd drive into an ambush and the lot of them would be wiped out.

Then he was startled by the thought that he was in love with Jean, that he'd do anything to save her life. If he didn't hurt so much, he'd laugh.

Maybe after all his mental threats against her, it was ridiculous to tell himself he was in love with her, but the fact remained that he would do anything to save her life. He guessed it was the first really decent idea he'd had for a long time.

Slowly he pulled himself to his knees, then on up until he was on his feet with his back to the wall. Turning, he glanced through the window and for an instant he was paralyzed, unable even to breathe. Indians were swarming out of the scrub oak and running toward the cabin.

Well, he'd take as many of them as he could, he told himself as he drew his gun. Apparently they decided from the way he had fallen that he was dead. Now they began to scatter, some running toward Armand's body and others toward Rafferty's that lay close to the barn. Two turned toward Lopez's body and two more came on toward the cabin.

He knocked the glass out of the window and fired at the two who were now not more than ten feet in front of him. He was shaky and weak and his shoulder hurt like hell. He should have got both of them dead center, but he hit one in the arm and apparently made a clean miss with the second shot.

The Indians darted around the corner. The one he'd hit hadn't been hurt very much, and he cursed his weakness. He saw that the other Indians were moving the three bodies toward the barn. He holstered his gun, feeling sweat run down his face. He wiped a hand across his forehead.

He wasn't thinking clearly, but he realized the Indians were getting the bodies out of sight so the stage driver would not be warned of what had happened. He knew, then, that his fears for Jean were as bad as he had thought. The renegades were waiting for the stage.

A moment later he saw the two Indians he had shot at cross the yard to the barn. He thought they might come into the cabin through the back door. He'd better drop the bar, he told himself, and started to cross the room.

Suddenly it was 1,000 miles across the room and he saw he wasn't going to make it. The blood had soaked the bandanna and was running down his side. He was going to bleed to death.

The walls started to turn, the floor rolled up in great waves in front of him, then his knees turned to rubber, and he fell, the last thought in his numbed brain one of complete failure. He would not be able to warn the stage.

XVI

Despite the tension that had drawn his nerves tight, the sleepless night caught up with Ollie again and his head tipped forward until his chin was against his chest. Presently his head began to roll back and forth with the lurching of the stage.

Jean put an arm around him and tried to draw his head toward her so he could lay it against her shoulder, but he was too tall for them to be comfortable in that position. She withdrew her arm, deciding his head would just have to roll.

The sun was noon high, the coach's short shadow running beside it on the edge of the road. The sky to the west was turning dark and Jean saw lightning flashes striking downward at the earth from the forbidding black bank of clouds. Occasionally she could hear the distant rumble of thunder somewhere back in the San Juans. The storm would hit them before they reached Durango, she thought.

Well, she wasn't afraid of thunderstorms, she told herself, but she was deathly afraid of Bronc Killion and the men who were riding with him. Her hands squeezed against the shoe box on her lap. So far she and Ollie had been lucky. Now, only a few hours out of Durango, she wondered if their luck would continue to hold.

She knew that Ollie, and probably McCoy and Ash, too, expected Killion to try again. The next few hours, then, would be the crucial ones.

Suddenly the coach began to slow down. Ollie woke and shook his head. He grinned ruefully at Jean as he rubbed the back of his neck. He said: "I can tell you one thing. This stagecoach isn't the best place in the world to sleep."

"I know," Jean said. "I tried to pull your head

over on to my shoulder, but it didn't work. You're too tall and we're too crowded."

The coach stopped. McCoy stepped down and opened the door on Ollie's side. He said: "Ida, your pa's coming. Al spotted him on the other side of the cañon we just pulled out of. He's a couple of miles back, but he's moving faster'n we are. What do you want to do?"

"I . . . I don't know," Ida said. "What do you think we'd better do?"

"I'm not scared of him," McCoy said. "If it was anybody else, I'd take care of him when he got here, but I don't want to kill your father. If he's crazy enough to chase us, he might start shooting when he gets close and somebody could get killed. We aren't far from Bear Creek station, but it's my guess he'll catch us before we get there."

For a moment no one said anything. Jean, glancing at Ollie, was afraid he would volunteer to get out and wait for Finley and stop him. He leaned forward, staring at McCoy. He said: "I'll wait here for him, Mike, and I'll stop him. I'll pound some sense into his head or I'll kill him."

Jean sighed, telling herself that she knew her future husband pretty well. She put a hand over his and squeezed. She wanted to tell him he couldn't do it, but she checked herself. Holding her tongue in such situations was something she had to learn.

"No, Mister Dutton," Ida said. "This is not your fight. If somebody else can take the coach into Durango, Mike and I will stay here and have it out with Pa."

This time Jean did not hold her tongue. The idea was so preposterous that she said before she thought: "You can't do that with Killion's gang around here and the renegade Indians somewhere in the country."

"That's right," Johnny Roan said. "I'll stop him. Ollie's got a lot of people depending on him getting to Durango in time. Mike, you can't let anyone else handle the lines and you know it, but, hell, nobody's depending on me for anything."

Roan stepped out of the coach in spite of Ida's objections. McCoy started to shake his head, then caught a signal in Ollie's eyes. He stepped back.

"All right, Johnny," McCoy said. "Handle it any way you have to. You know what the old booger's like."

"Thank you, Johnny," Ida said. "He is my father, but none of you except Mike know the kind of father he's been. If you have to kill him, I wouldn't hold it against you."

McCoy shut the door. "My thanks, too, Johnny. Chances are we'll see you at Bear Creek station. If we're gone when you get there, the Browns will put you up until the next stage comes through."

"Sure." Roan took a hitch on his belt and tipped

his hat back on his forehead with his thumb. "Get moving, Mike." He turned his gaze to Sally who was watching him with close attention. "So long, Sally," Roan said. "Think of me while I'm dreaming about you."

"Of course I'll think about you," Sally said.

McCoy was back in the high seat now. He cracked the whip and the coach rolled again. Ida said miserably: "I'll never forgive myself if Pa kills him."

"He won't," Ollie said.

"I don't understand this, I guess," Sally said.

"Johnny's past is his own business," Ollie told her. "Maybe the gossip about him in Durango was just gossip, but he was supposed to have been with the Stockton gang when they were raising Cain around town. He wanted a chance to do something worthwhile that would rub out the gossip. I thought he deserved it."

"Of course he deserved it," Sally said. "I . . . I didn't know about the gossip."

"Most of all, Sally," Jean said, "he supposed you knew what the gossip was and he wanted you to think well of him."

"I do already," Sally said. "I like him. He's changed since he got on the stage in Alamosa. He was such a smart aleck at first."

"He has changed," Ollie agreed, "and maybe you're the reason. It strikes me that he's done a lot of growing up since we left . . ."

He stopped when Horn held up a hand. Horn said: "I've been hearing gunshots somewhere ahead of us. I'm not sure what it means, but I don't like it."

McCoy must have heard it, too. His whip cracked and the horses quickened their pace. Jean gripped Ollie's hand, her eyes searching his face. He was staring at the side of the hill above the road, his expression grim, his body tense.

One of two things was happening, Ollie thought. Killion's gang or the Indians were attacking the Bear Creek station. Either one could mean disaster for everyone in the coach, and for Johnny Roan, too.

XVII

The shooting had stopped. Ollie didn't know what it meant, but, in a way, he wished the firing had continued. At least Mike McCoy would have known what was happening at Bear Creek station when he drove into the clearing.

When they entered the clearing a few minutes later, Ollie could not see that anything was wrong. A small column of smoke was visible in the sultry air above the chimney. No one was in sight. In spite of the apparently peaceful scene, the tension in Ollie grew.

His gaze swept the scrub oak to the south, the creek beyond the buildings, the scattered timber to the north. Nowhere could Ollie see a solitary thing that was out of place, but the feeling of impending trouble grew. It was the very peacefulness of the scene in front of them that was wrong. Old man Fields, the stock tender, should have been waiting in front of the cabin to take the horses. Mr. Brown would have been outside, waiting to greet the passengers. Mrs. Brown might be inside, hurrying with the food, but no one was outside the house.

Ollie called: "Mike, something's wrong!"

"I know it," McCoy called back, "but what?"

As if in answer to McCoy's question, a man appeared behind the cabin. He was hurt or sick. He put out a hand against the wall to hold himself upright and yelled something. He motioned with his free hand for the stage to wheel in behind the cabin.

The stage was making too much racket and the man, hurt or sick, hadn't yelled loud enough to be heard. McCoy at least had sensed a warning. He shouted—"Hang on!"—and put the horses into a hard run, angling off the road through the sagebrush toward the rear of the cabin.

The instant the coach left the road, Ollie heard a yell of rage and disappointment from the scrub oak. An instant later a ragged volley exploded from the brush. Ollie saw the flashes of powder flame and the black smoke; he heard the roar of guns as bullets snapped overhead.

"Down!" Ollie yelled at the girls.

Ollie started to draw his gun and pulled his hand away at once, knowing that it would only be a waste of lead to shoot from here. The girls hunkered down as much as they could, Horn shielding their bodies with his on the side the bullets were coming from. There was little protection in the coach, and, if the distance hadn't been great, everybody would have been wounded or killed before McCoy reached the cabin.

Someone on top was shooting back, then Ollie heard one of the men on top yell: "I'm hit." A few seconds later they were safe for the moment, the cabin between the stage and the riflemen in the scrub oak.

Ollie was the first out of the coach when it stopped. He saw that it was Bronc Killion who had warned them. The outlaw was leaning against the log wall, his face gray and drawn, a dark blood stain down the left side of his shirt.

"Indians," Killion said in a hoarse voice. "They got my men and shot hell out of me."

Ollie saw that Al Ash was helping Ted Conner down off the top of the coach. Horn was on the ground now, and Ollie called to the girls: "Get inside!"

He ran into the cabin and through the back room. He crossed the front room, shut the door, and barred it, noticing the pool of blood on the floor. He glanced through the window, thinking that, if the Indians rushed them now, they'd be here before any resistance could be organized. But no one was in sight between the cabin and the scrub oak. The firing had stopped as soon as the coach wheeled behind the cabin.

Horn and Ash had helped Conner to the bed in the back room. Sally and Ida were there, Ida saying: "Here, let me see what I can do for him."

"You can't do nothing." Conner saw Ollie and motioned for him to come closer. When Ollie leaned over him, the dying man said: "I'm glad I ain't going back to tell my wife I couldn't get any money. I ain't leaving her nothing, Ollie. Nothing at all. Would you see how she's making out?"

"I'll see her," Ollie promised.

Conner seemed relieved. He closed his eyes. Blood had spread over his chest and stomach, and Ollie, looking down at him, sensed that he welcomed death, that it was the only way out for a man who had been a failure at everything he had ever tried, including marriage.

"The damned fool committed suicide," Ash said. "As soon as the shooting started, he yanked his six-shooter out of his holster and started firing away. If he'd stayed down, they might not have hit him. He was too far away to do any good with a revolver. Besides, he couldn't see anything to shoot at."

"Watch from the front window, Al," Ollie said. "They might decide to come at us."

"I'll watch," Ash said, "but these Paiutes don't

have the guts to attack us. They're the skulking kind."

Ollie turned away as Ida pulled a blanket over Conner's body.

"Stay on the floor," Ollie told Sally and Ida. "If they see anybody at a window, they'll start shooting again."

Jean still wasn't with the other girls. Wondering why she hadn't come in, Ollie stepped through the back door. Bronc Killion lay on the ground, a hand clutching his blood-soaked shirt. Jean sat beside him, holding his other hand. When she saw Ollie, she motioned to him, saying softly: "He's got something to tell you."

Ollie hesitated, staring at Killion's gray face that had the look of death upon it. He said: "I guess he just wants me to know he's working for Billy Bellew."

"I reckon you knew that without me telling you," Killion said. His voice was so low that Ollie barely heard him. "You fooled me pretty good when we held you up. We aimed to try again when you got here."

"Where's the Browns?" Ollie asked. "And old man Fields?"

"Missus Brown's in Durango," Killion said. "We killed Brown and Fields. We figured we'd get you when you stopped in front of the cabin, but the Indians got us first."

Justice, Ollie thought. He started to turn away.

There was too much to be done to waste time listening to what Bronc Killion had aimed to do and very likely would have done if the Indians had not taken a hand.

"Wait, Dutton," Killion said. "There's something you need to know. Bellew aren't gonna let you get to Durango with that *dinero*. That's why Horn's on the stage with you. If I don't stop you, he's supposed to."

So now it was out in the open at last. Horn had denied it, but Ollie hadn't believed him. Still, Ollie had been willing to let the fiction stand until Horn had made a move. Now he was somewhere behind Ollie. If Horn wanted to shoot him in the back, there didn't seem there was much Ollie could do. That was just about what Horn would do, now that Killion had named him.

Ollie hesitated only a second. If he was going down, he'd do it with his gun in his hand. He wheeled to face Horn, sweeping his revolver from the holster as he made his turn. He froze, the gun barrel not quite level. Ed Horn stood with his hands in the air, a thin smile on his lips.

"Hold it, Dutton," Horn said. "I'm not pulling a gun on you. Not with a dozen renegade Indians out yonder in the brush. We need each other for a while yet."

It was true. Ollie had been very much aware of that, but he had not expected Horn to stand pat. He said: "Later, then?"

205

Horn nodded, the smile still on his lips. "Later. I guess you knew all the time why I was on the coach. I didn't figure you believed what I told you when we started, but I hoped Killion could pull it off and I'd be able to stay out of it. Now I guess it's up to me to see that *dinero* doesn't get to Durango."

Ollie holstered his gun.

McCoy said: "I'm glad we got that settled. Looked for a while that you two roosters didn't have enough sense to declare a truce."

"I'm taking that money to Durango," Ollie said. "If you're going to stop me, Horn, this is good a time as any."

"No," Horn said. "I'd rather fail and have Bellew blackball me all through the San Juans than to let the Paiutes have our scalps, so I say we wait."

"We're still four hours out of Durango, Ollie," McCoy said.

"You're saying you don't see how I'm gonna get to Durango in time?" Ollie asked. "That it?"

"That's exactly what I'm saying," McCoy agreed. "I'm guessing it's part of the reason Horn don't want no trouble with you. He figures you're whipped now."

"Correct," Horn said, his grin broader now. "You'll never make it. We're pinned down till we get help, and that isn't gonna come for a day or more. Why should we shoot each other?"

"We'll see," Ollie said sourly, knowing that Horn might be right. "What about after it's dark?" Ollie asked McCoy.

"They aren't gonna get proddy after dark," McCoy said, "but along about daylight we may see something."

Ollie turned back to Jean.

"He's dead," Jean said. "Seems funny, but he told me he stayed alive to warn us about the Indians. He said he fainted and didn't know how long he lay on the floor, then he came to and he said he knew he had to get out back of the cabin and warn us." She paused, and then asked: "He did save our lives, didn't he?"

Ollie nodded. It was true. If the stage had come on in and stopped in front of the cabin, the chances were everyone in the coach would have been killed or wounded. Now, looking down at Killion's face, so utterly barren in death, Ollie felt his hatred for the man die. In spite of all that Killion had intended doing, Ollie couldn't hate a man who had saved all of them except Ted Conner.

XVIII

As Ollie had thought, there was much to be done. The dead men were moved to a small lean-to room that had been used by the Browns for a store room. As soon as Al Ash was relieved at the window, he brought the treasure box in from the coach. Ollie started a fire in the big range and the girls, searching the pantry, found the makings of a meal. McCoy managed to get the horses to the barn, and was standing watch there.

The men barred both doors and, finding heavy shutters in the store room, placed them over all of the windows except the one at the back. Fortunately two buckets of water had been carried to the cabin from the creek and left on a shelf behind the stove. The reservoir, too, was full, so for the moment water was not an immediate problem. Neither was food, Jean told Ollie.

The only problem as far as time was concerned was the delivery of the money to the Syndicate in Durango. The more Ollie thought about it, the more he realized that he faced an impossible situation. Horn had been right about help not coming until at least a day had passed, perhaps two. The stage company's agent in Durango would not be concerned about McCoy's failure to arrive on time, at least not for several hours, perhaps for a full day.

A number of things could delay the coach, and the agent might wait until morning before informing the sheriff, or the soldiers at Fort Lewis. If he thought the Indians had caused the delay, that was what he would probably do.

As they ate dinner, Ollie became so furious at Horn's smirking attitude of triumph that he had all he could do to keep from slapping the grin off his face. As far as Ed Horn was concerned, the game was won, and Ollie, searching his mind for a solution to his problem, could not come up with anything that held the slightest promise of success.

McCoy could bring the horses from the barn and hook up to the coach, but he'd be under heavy fire the instant he drove past the cabin and into view of the Indians in the scrub oak. Ollie was fully aware that McCoy and Ash and the passengers had been lucky coming in, with no one getting hurt except Ted Conner. They could not expect to be that lucky again.

The only other possibility was to wait until after dark, but the Paiutes would not overlook that possibility. They'd be waiting somewhere to the west, probably where the road dipped down to cross the creek. The bank was steep enough to make the stage almost stop. He would have to ease down to the water carefully. When he did that, the Indians would swarm over the coach.

If all the passengers had been men, Ollie would have tried to talk to McCoy and persuade him to attempt the night run, but with three women in the coach Ollie wouldn't even suggest it. Then Ollie considered taking the money and trying to get through on foot, but the odds of him getting past the Indians were slim. Four or five men could fight the Paiutes off, but one man wouldn't have a chance with them.

Even if he honestly felt he could get through alone, Ollie could not leave Jean. Saving the Katydid was important, but it was nothing compared to Jean's life or even her peace of mind. He had put her through enough since asking her to make this trip. He would not desert her now.

Ed Horn had left the table and gone to the front window. The shutter had been placed so there was a narrow crack at one side through which a man could watch the scrub oak. Now Horn was intensely studying the brush.

Ida went to the back window to see if Johnny Roan and her father were in sight. She stood there, straight-backed and rigid. Looking at her, Ollie thought he knew how she felt. By coming on the stage, she had brought additional danger to them, at least to Johnny Roan. Too, she was concerned about McCoy, out there in the barn by himself. Suddenly her shoulders slumped and she began to cry.

"I'll bring some grub out to Mike," Ollie said. "There's a little rise between here and the oak brush. If I stay flat on my belly, they sure won't have much to shoot at."

Jean opened her mouth to object, then looked at Ida's back and decided not to say a word. She found an empty flour sack in the pantry and returned to the table, saying: "Sally, find a quart jar and pour what's left of the coffee into it. I'll fix the meat and biscuits."

Sally rose and left the table. Ollie leaned forward and said in a low tone to Ash: "I guess it isn't a secret now that the *dinero* is in Jean's lunch box. If I don't make it, but if the stage gets to Durango in time, give her a hand. The money has got to be in Judge Lorne's office by twelve noon. Bellew will be standing there with a watch in his hand. You can count on it."

"You'll make it," Ash said, "but I'll do what I can if you don't." He paused and shot a glance at Ed Horn's back. "Only I don't figure the stage will get to Durango in time."

"The Indians might be gone by morning," Ollie said.

Ash shook his head. "Not unless they take some kind of a beating. They're like wolves that hang around a herd of cattle when the feed's been poor for a while, or kill a fawn the mother hid out. They know that sooner or later we'll make a break for it, unless help comes, which isn't likely for a while. When we do make a break, they'll have us."

Ollie rose, thinking that Ash was exactly right. He took the sack and the jar, tossed his hat onto the bed as he crossed the back room, and lifted the bar. "Put the bar back as soon as I'm out," he told Jean, "and don't let anybody in unless you know who it is."

"If you get to the barn, I guess you can get back," she said, and kissed him. "God keep you."

He opened the door and stepped outside. He dropped on his hands and knees before he reached the corner of the cabin and started the long crawl to the barn. He had little hope they wouldn't spot him. If they did and started shooting, he'd make a run for it. A fast-moving man would be harder to hit than one flat on his belly crawling across the yard at a snail's pace.

One thing in his favor was the fact that the light was very thin. The black clouds had moved in from the west and thunder was a steady rumble. The smell of rain had been in the air for some time, but so far not a drop had fallen from the low-hanging, ominous clouds.

He inched across the yard, the sack in one hand, the jar in the other. He was afraid that even at his pace and being as careful as he was, he would raise enough dust to give himself away. But he kept moving and they didn't see him, so perhaps the dust was not visible in the poor light.

He eased around rocks if he saw them in time, and, when he didn't, they gouged him when he let his weight down. He worked his way around clumps of cacti, their sharp barbs seeming to reach out to stab him.

Then the rain hit before he had covered half the distance to the barn, as suddenly and violently as if a celestial bucket had been tipped over. The effect was that of drawing a silver curtain across the clearing.

McCoy must have been watching him. Now he yelled: "Run for it, Ollie!"

Ollie was already on his feet, his boots churning into the dust that turned to mud before he reached the barn. McCoy had the door open and shut it the instant Ollie was inside.

"Now why in the hell are you out here risking a hole in your hide?" McCoy demanded.

Ollie wiped a forearm across his face. "It wasn't real smart, was it?"

"Smart?" McCoy shouted. "It was plain stupid. They aren't gonna bother me till night. When it's good and dark, they'll maybe make a play for the horses, but by that time you could have walked across the yard."

"I came because Ida got worried and thought you were thirsty and starving to death," Ollie said, and held the sack and jar out to him.

McCoy took them, his face turning red. He grinned a little as he said: "Well, to tell the truth, I was getting a little hungry."

XIX

Ollie was soaked to the skin in the short time he was in the open. He took his clothes off and wrung out all the water that he could. By the time he was dressed again, the rain had stopped and the sun was shining.

McCoy had been eating ravenously. Now he

said: "Look at that. The storm's over. Isn't this the damnedest country?"

The sky to the east was dark now, and thunder rumbled from the direction of the Continental Divide. Ollie nodded, having seen many such violent and sudden storms at this altitude.

"I had another reason for coming, Mike," Ollie said. "I didn't figure you'd come to the cabin and I wanted to talk to you."

McCoy grinned and patted his stomach. "Well, I feel better. I've been fretting about you risking your hide just to keep me from getting hungry, but now you say you want to talk. You're right about me not going to the cabin. Them damned renegades want our horses whether they get our scalps or not, and I'm not gonna let 'em have 'em. We need them horses to pull that coach into Durango or we might sit here for a week. They got away with all the horses that were here. Leastwise, I haven't seen 'em."

"I can't sit here for a week," Ollie said. "We've got to figure out some way to get to Durango by noon tomorrow."

McCoy finished the coffee and put the jar down. "If you think I'm gonna hitch up and pull out of here . . ."

"No," Ollie broke in. "Sure, I thought of that. I even thought of trying it after dark. I figured I might try going through by myself. None of my ideas is worth a damn. All I know is that if we aren't rolling by at least seven in the morning, I won't be in Durango in time."

"You'd better say six," McCoy said. "It's a four-hour run in dry weather, but after a rain like the one we just had, the creeks will be up and there's a few places where the road muds up awful bad. I'm not even sure we can make it in six hours."

Ollie threw out his hands in despair. "What am I going to do? I can't let Bellew and the Syndicate win by default. I've got the money. That was the part that worried me when I started. You know how many people are depending on me to save the Katydid. My partners, Pete Risley and Duke Warren. Even Johnny Roan asked me for a job. Mike, I've got to get there."

McCoy shook his head. "I don't know what to do. They might be gone by morning, but there's no way to know until we start. If we traveled fifty yards and no shots were fired, we'd be purty safe in figuring they was gone, but before we went that fifty yards, they'd cut us to ribbons."

"They didn't when we came in," Ollie said.

"They were surprised," McCoy said. "They expected us to pull up in front of the cabin and we'd be sitting ducks for 'em, but when we angled off the road and headed for the back side of the cabin, we fooled 'em. Besides, we were moving real good. We won't be rolling like that in this mud."

Ollie paced back and forth in the runway behind

the stalls. He'd dreamed his dreams before he'd left Durango along with Pete Risley and Duke Warren. He'd had a few bad hours in Denver before he had raised the money, but once it was in his leather bag, he'd had every right to think his dreams were going to pan out. Now the prospect of failure was more than he could stand.

It would have been understandable if the failure had been due to Bronc Killion's pack of outlaws. Or some sly trick of Ed Horn's. But neither was true. He was pinned down by a band of flea-bitten, no-good, thieving Paiutes who happened to be in the country at this particular time and who had no concern whatever with the Katydid.

Something Al Ash had said about the Paiutes came into his mind. He asked: "Al's younger'n me, isn't he?"

McCoy nodded. "He's my age, but what's that got to do with it? He's a smart *hombre*, and he's got all the guts in the world."

"Sure, sure," Ollie said impatiently. "I'm not running him down, but what I want to know is how come he's got so much savvy of these Paiutes. He was saying they're dangerous like wolves that hang around a herd of cattle that's been on poor feed, or kill a helpless fawn. He said they'd get out and leave us alone if they took some kind of a beating."

"They're dangerous as hell," McCoy said sharply as if he thought Ollie was inferring they weren't. "Sure, they're cowards, but sitting yonder in that scrub oak, they aren't risking anything. All they've got to do is to pull their triggers, and, by glory, that's what they'll do if they get a bead on any of us. These boogers don't have no conscience. I'd rather take my chances with a war party of Sioux or Cheyennes than these . . ."

"Mike, I know that," Ollie said impatiently. "I'm asking you if Al knows what he's talking about. I mean, he's no mountain man. How can he be so sure what these Paiutes are like and what they'll do? I can tell you about Utes or the Arapahoes . . ."

"He ought to know about 'em," McCoy broke in. "He's a Mormon. He was raised in Utah. He's known the Paiutes ever since he could walk. Why, hell, he's hunted with 'em. For all I know, he's helped 'em steal horses. They're the biggest damn' thieves in the world. Now he couldn't tell you nothing about Arapahoes, but when it comes to the Paiutes . . ."

"All right, all right," Ollie said, excitement beginning to rush through him. "Then they would slope out of here if they took some kind of a beating, like if we carried the fight to them?"

"Sure they would," McCoy answered, "but if you think we're gonna carry the fight to them, you're crazy. They're hell on high, red wheels with a knife. They'd cut us to pieces."

"But if it did happen," Ollie asked, "you'd hightail out of here before sunup?"

"Sure I would," McCoy said, "but who's gonna carry the fight to them?"

"I am," Ollie said.

"Commit suicide at your age?" McCoy asked. "With Jean coming this far with you to marry you? Man, you must be crazy. The Katydid isn't worth it."

"Maybe not," Ollie said, "but that's the deal."

McCoy stared at him as if he thought Ollie had gone out of his mind. He opened his mouth to continue the argument when a burst of gunfire broke out from the scrub oak. "Now what?" McCoy shouted. He ran outside, Ollie behind him.

Johnny Roan was coming in on a horse, a big black. He was riding low and making no effort to shoot back at the Indians. He had the horse in a hard run and was coming straight toward the barn. Ollie pulled his gun and wheeled toward the scrub oak. Standing close to the wall, he began firing. He couldn't see anybody, but he shot at the flashes of powder flame. An instant later McCoy was firing, and then Ash and Horn cut loose from the house.

The Indians kept up a sporadic fire, but the shots from the barn and house must have disconcerted them. Whether it was true or not, Johnny Roan reached the barn and rode through the door and tumbled out of his saddle onto the litter that covered the floor.

McCoy and Ollie ran to him. He sat up and leaned against the wall, a hand pressed to his side. "I got it just before you fellows started to burn a little powder," he said. "I don't think it's bad, but it hurts like hell."

"Look at him," McCoy said. "I'll take care of his horse."

"Pull off your shirt," Ollie said. "Your under-shirt, too."

Roan obeyed. Ollie saw that the bullet had struck a rib on his right side and gouged out a furrow in the flesh. It was a shallow wound and it wasn't bleeding much, but Roan probably felt as if he'd been hit by a sledge-hammer.

"Not much we can do for it," Ollie said. "You'd better lie down and grit your teeth."

McCoy brought the saddle blanket and spread it in the runway. Roan didn't argue. He put his undershirt on and lay down. He said: "Pa Finley's dead, Mike. I killed him. I didn't aim to, but he was drunk and mean. He wouldn't listen to anything I said. I think he'd have killed Ida if he'd had a chance."

McCoy's face turned grave. "I'm glad it wasn't me who done it. He was an animal, but I still didn't want to kill him."

"I was waiting for him in the middle of the road," Johnny said. "I had my gun on him and I made him get off his horse, and then I tried to tell him he ought to turn around and go back. I said Ida was eighteen and old enough to do what she damned pleased. I said he was getting a good son-in-law, but he was out of his mind. He cussed me and Ida and you, and finally he told me to get out of his way or he'd kill me. When I didn't move, he pulled his gun on me."

"There aren't many people gonna weep over him," McCoy said. "Not even his own daughters. That's a bad way to die, everybody glad you're gone."

"I was fetching his body on the horse," Roan said, "but when I got to the edge of the timber, I figured the Indians had pinned you down. I'd heard the shooting when you got here and I'd seen the coach back of the cabin, so I took him off the horse and got into the saddle and come on. He isn't far, but if we leave him, the coyotes will chew him to pieces."

"We'll fetch him as soon as it's dark," McCoy said. "We're gonna have to stay here in the barn till dark, too."

Roan shut his eyes and gritted his teeth. "It'll be a long, tough ride to Durango, but maybe I'll be healed up before we can start."

"No you won't," Ollie said. "We're leaving before sunup in the morning."

He carried his knife in a scabbard on his left hip. Now he squatted in the runway and, drawing his knife, began to whet it on the side of his boot.

"Tell him good bye, Johnny," McCoy said. "You're looking at a man who's hell-bent on committing suicide. He says he's going after the Indians."

"No, I'm not committing suicide," Ollie said. "I'm just aiming to get us out of here in the morning."

"Maybe you can talk him out of it," McCoy said.

"Not me," Roan said. "I'd go with him if I didn't have this bullet hole."

Ollie kept on whetting the knife and didn't look at Roan, but he felt a great warmth of satisfaction. Johnny Roan had come a long way since he'd first boarded the stage in Alamosa.

XX

When the dusk light had thinned so that the Paiutes couldn't shoot with any degree of accuracy, McCoy helped Johnny Roan into the cabin without drawing any fire from the scrub oak. Ollie stayed in the barn with the horses. McCoy and Ed Horn brought Pa Finley's body in and left it in the lean-to room with the others. By that time supper was ready and McCoy ate before he returned to the barn.

"Ida didn't even want to look at her pa," McCoy told Ollie. "She said he had never brought her anything but pain and sorrow as long as she could remember." McCoy swallowed, and then burst out: "Ollie, that is one hell of a memory to have of your father. My dad used to beat the tar out of me, but I always deserved it and I knew he loved me. When he died, I felt like a part of me had gone with him."

Ollie nodded, knowing exactly what McCoy meant. He said: "Ida's got you. That's more'n the other three girls have."

"That's right. I'll make her happy, too." McCoy hesitated, then he said: "Supper's ready. Better go eat. I don't look for no trouble till morning."

"We won't have no trouble then, either," Ollie said.

McCoy grabbed his arm. "You aren't gonna go on with that hare-brained scheme of yours, are you?"

"Sure I am," Ollie said. "Be careful who you're shooting at tonight. It might be me."

McCoy dropped his hand and grunted in disgust. "All right. Go ahead. I never got anywhere arguing with a mule."

Ollie stepped outside and McCoy closed and latched the door on the inside. For a time Ollie stood beside the barn, studying the clearing to the south. It was dark now, but the sky was still clear and the stars seemed unusually bright and numerous. The scrub oak was swallowed by the darkness, but Ollie could see the faint glow of a campfire somewhere behind the fringe of brush.

He was thoughtful as he crossed the yard to the cabin. Probably most of the Indians would be at the fire, but they would have guards out and these were the men he would kill. He had to find them one at a time. He knew he couldn't slip through the scrub oak without warning them of his presence. The brush was too thick; there were too many dried leaves on the ground that would rustle as he wormed his way through the oak.

He tapped on the back door, calling: "It's Ollie!"

The door opened at once. He stepped inside, the door was closed and barred, and Jean turned to face him. She said: "I've been waiting right here ever since Mike left. You're not going out there tonight."

"Yes, I'm going." He took her hands and drew her toward him. "Honey, there has to be a division of authority in every family. I don't figure I'll tell you what to cook for supper or which dress to wear to a party, but there's some decisions I've got to make. This is one."

She tipped her head back to look at him, then managed a smile. "I know, Ollie. This is the kind of mistake I made in the first place. I learned my lesson, but I seem to keep forgetting it. Come on. Your supper's ready."

Johnny Roan was lying on the bed, his head propped up on one arm, a broad grin on his face.

He said: "You got out of that pretty lucky, Ollie. It'll be different after you're married."

"You hush up, Johnny Roan," Jean scolded. "I don't want him thinking about that until after I have him roped and tied."

As Ollie ate, Al Ash sat down across the table from him with a cup of coffee, but Ed Horn remained in his chair at the other end of the room. He made no effort to be friendly. As long as the Paiutes were doing his job for him, Horn had been pleasant and relaxed, but now the thought that Ollie was taking the fight to them and maybe prompting their withdrawal was not to his liking.

Ash said nothing until Ollie finished eating, then he asked: "You're bound to go out there?"

Ollie nodded. "You think of anything better?"

"No, though I figure anything would be better," Ash answered sourly. "Just one piece of advice. Don't let 'em take you prisoner. They're scavengers, but that don't make no difference. They can have a hell of a lot of fun with you if they take you alive."

"I'll see they don't," Ollie said.

"When are you going?"

"Now," Ollie answered. "I thought this was the time they'd be the least likely to expect anything to happen. Along toward sunup they'll figure on us rolling the stage out of here and they'll be watching for us."

"That's right." Ash held out his hand as Ollie rose. "Good luck."

"Thanks," Ollie said.

Horn did not so much as nod. Jean walked with him to the door. Johnny Roan sat up in bed and held out his hand.

"Ollie," the boy said, "I figure you'll be knocking on the door again purty soon, but, in case you don't, I want you to know that it's meant a hell of a lot to me to have been treated like an honest man from the time we left Alamosa. It's more'n Billy Bellew ever done."

"It was the only way to treat you," Ollie said as he shook hands. "And I'll be back pretty soon."

He turned to the door. Jean put her hands on his shoulders and looked up at him. "I'm trying hard not to cry," she whispered. "It's strange, but you don't really know how much you love a person until you come to a time like this."

"Maybe it's a good thing to have a time like this once in a while," he said.

He kissed her, then held her so that her face was pressed against his chest for a moment. He knew what she was thinking, that his life was more important than all the mines in the San Juan, but that was not the way he looked at it.

Ollie had seen his friends, Pete Risley and Duke Warren, work for day's wages in the mines and try to support a family, and he had seen what it had done to them and their wives and children.

He did not propose for Jean to live the way the Warren and Risley women had lived.

He released her and lifted the bar to open the door. He stepped outside and around the corner of the building. There he stopped, glancing at the stars. None was visible. He was surprised to find that the clouds had swept across the sky again.

For a time he didn't move, thinking that in one way he was glad the night had turned so black. It gave him a better chance to get to the Indians without being detected, but there was the other side to it, too. In darkness as complete as this, he might stumble onto one or more of the Paiutes before he realized it.

He could still see the dim glow of the Indians' campfire and once more he told himself it would be suicide to try to work his way through the scrub oak. In any case, he did not want to tangle with the entire pack of them. The trick, then, was to try to find one or two who were watching the cabin and barn.

A prickle slid down Ollie's spine as he considered this. He might stumble into one of them out there within fifty feet of the barn. If not there, then certainly farther on where the road crossed the creek.

Ollie drew his knife and started toward the stream, moving swiftly and silently. A few times he wandered off the road into the sagebrush, then immediately dropped belly-flat and waited. He had made enough noise brushing against the stubby clumps of sage to give himself away if an Indian was near. Apparently none was, and, after listening several minutes and hearing nothing, he went on.

He was within fifty feet of the creek when he paused, then dropped into the grass between the wheel ruts of the road. He thought he heard something ahead of him, perhaps a moccasin dislodging a stone along the creek. He couldn't see anything move, but he sensed the presence of an Indian and a moment later caught the brave's gamy smell.

He heard the Indian climb up the east bank, rattling rocks and creating small slides of loose dirt. A moment later Ollie made out the man's shadowy shape moving toward him. He tensed, ready to lunge upward from his position in the grass, but the Indian stopped and stood motionlessly.

Perhaps he was listening, or maybe he was undecided about what he should do next. Ollie had no way of knowing, but he guessed the brave had been ordered to slip up close to the cabin or barn, and now he may have decided it was a stupid risk for him to take when all that he and his friends had to do was to wait.

The Indian suddenly turned back toward the creek. Ollie had been afraid the sound of his breathing would give him away, but his presence had gone undetected. Now he came up out of the grass in a long lunge, knowing he would never have a better opportunity than this.

The Paiute must have heard him. He started to turn, but he was too late. Ollie's left arm caught him directly under his chin and locked against his windpipe, shutting off his air. Ollie's right hand with the knife swept out and in, plunging the steel into the brave's belly. Ollie yanked the blade free and struck again and again, then released the body, and slipped back from the creek.

Ollie realized he had made some noise. So had the dead Indian in the scuffle, enough noise to bring two more Paiutes scrambling up the bank. He couldn't take both of them with his knife, and in the darkness a gun was useless, so he hugged the ground in the sagebrush beside the road.

He heard the low mutter of their talk when they found their dead friend. He didn't know their language, but from their tone he judged they were frightened.

They had no way of knowing how many white men were hiding out here in the darkness. All they knew for sure was that one of their number had died with a knife in his belly, a fate that might be waiting for them. They didn't tarry. They dragged their dead companion toward the creek and a moment later Ollie heard the faint *click* of hoofs on stones beside the stream, then the sound died.

Ollie waited for what seemed to be hours,

although he knew it could not have been that long. He was convinced there were no more guards here at the crossing, and he still could not get at their camp. Even if he did, he could not accomplish anything. Turning, he walked back to the cabin and around it to the back door and tapped, calling: "It's Ollie!"

Immediately the door was flung open and Jean stood there with her arms extended, tears running down her cheeks. She cried—"Ollie, Ollie!"—and hugged him. Sally and Ida ran to him and Al Ash was there, too, grinning at him, and Johnny Roan, sitting on the edge of the bed, lifted a hand in salutation as he said: "You're a good man, Ollie."

Horn appeared in the doorway leading into the front room and stood there, scowling. Ollie laughed. He said: "Horn, we're leaving before sunup and we'll have that *dinero* in Judge Lorne's hands by noon."

"You'll never make it," Horn said harshly. "Billy Bellew will never give that mine up."

"You say we're leaving?" Jean asked. "You mean you killed all . . . ?"

"Not all," Ollie said, "but we're leaving just the same. If anybody figures he'll be safer staying here, that's his privilege."

Al Ash saw the blood stain on Ollie's pants where he had wiped his knife. He said: "I don't think we'll have any trouble. I've got a hunch the road's clear all the way to Durango."

XXI

Breakfast was a silent meal eaten by lamplight. Ollie was not certain that the road to Durango was open despite Al Ash's assurance. Still, no one wanted to stay here in the Bear Creek station.

Later McCoy and Ollie hitched up the horses, loaded the stage, and with the first opalescent dawn light showing in the sky above the Continental Divide, McCoy drove the big coach out from behind the cabin.

The men held their guns in their hands. Johnny Roan, too, although his side was giving him fits. McCoy made no effort to travel fast, knowing he had to cross the creek slowly and that he couldn't outrun the Indians if they were planning an attack.

It took no more than five minutes to reach the creek and ease down the east bank and ford the water that was running high after the rain yesterday, but to everyone in the coach those five minutes were an eternity. There was no sound, no movement, no murderous rifle fire from ambush, and then the stage was across the creek and McCoy cracked his whip, and the coach picked up speed.

Jean held Ollie's hand after he holstered his gun and relaxed in his seat. Both Ida and Sally were pale-faced, but aside from that the girls gave no sign of the fear that had been in them. Johnny Roan gritted his teeth against the pain that racked his body at every jolt the coach gave him. Only Ed Horn seemed worried, his speculative gaze on Ollie.

"Don't try anything when we get to Durango, Horn," Ollie said. "No sense getting yourself killed pulling Billy Bellew's chestnuts out of the fire."

"I'll hold him off your back," Johnny said. "I may be half dead, but I'll do it so you can settle with Bellew. He blackballed me around Durango so I couldn't get a job in any of the mines. He started the talk about me being an outlaw and there never was anything to it."

"Why did he blackball you?" Sally asked.

"I got smart with him once," Johnny said. "You don't get smart with Billy Bellew, leastwise not a whippersnapper of a kid like me."

That, Ollie thought, was indeed the truth. Billy Bellew was not a man to get smart with.

McCoy had been right about the extra time it would take to reach Durango. They forded streams that were high and roily, they labored through mud, but they made it, rolling into Durango fifteen minutes before noon, too close for comfort, but still in time.

As they passed a row of cribs at the edge of town, Ollie saw Ted Conner's widow standing in a doorway. It hadn't taken her long to return to her old profession, Ollie thought. She had not been willing to give Conner a chance to get a grubstake. Perhaps he had known that, and so had preferred death to what he knew he would find when he got back to Durango.

Ollie glanced at Sally, wondering about her lieutenant and hoping that Johnny Roan would have a chance with her. Then the stage wheeled in close to the boardwalk and stopped, and Ollie had no time to think about the other passengers. He stepped out and gave Jean a hand, saying: "Wait five minutes." She nodded understanding.

Ollie stood there until Johnny Roan was out of the coach, his .45 in his hand. When Horn swung down, Johnny rammed the gun into his back. He said: "Make one wrong move, mister, and I'll let you have it."

But Ed Horn was not the formidable, cold-blooded, tough Syndicate man Ollie had judged him to be, at least not with the muzzle of Johnny's gun jammed against his spine. Billy Bellew stood in front of Judge Lorne's office up the street, and now Horn, seeing him, yelled: "He's got the money!"

Bellew didn't move. Ollie started toward him as a tall lieutenant left the stage office with a young woman. Ollie caught something about Sally's meeting his wife and he knew that Johnny Roan would have his chance. Ollie had thought it was this way, but he had not been well enough acquainted with the personnel at Fort Lewis to be sure.

Bellew stood motionless as a statue, waiting, a squat man with wide shoulders and a jutting jaw. Ollie had never known him to compromise or back down, once he had taken a position, and now, staring at this man who had hired an outlaw gang to hold up the stage and put every person on it in danger for no better reason than to keep Ollie and his friends from making good on an agreement that had been reached months ago, Ollie felt a wave of murderous hatred he had never felt for any other man, not even Bronc Killion.

"Make your play, Bellew!" Ollie called.

To his surprise Bellow swung around and strode into Judge Lorne's office. Ollie followed. Lorne sat at his desk, staring at Ollie over his steel-rimmed spectacles. Warren and Risley stood against the wall, Warren asking: "You get it, Ollie?"

"I got it," Ollie said, looking at Lorne. "You got the papers ready for us to sign, Judge?"

"They're ready," the lawyer said, "but according to the agreement . . ."

"It's past time by my watch," Bellew broke in. "They lost the Katydid right now. It reverts to the Syndicate."

"Now wait a minute . . . !" Risley shouted.

Lorne held up a hand. He said: "Billy, you've thrown your weight around this camp for quite a while, but setting the clock ahead to get what you want is going too far." He nodded at the Seth

Thomas clock hanging on the opposite wall. "We'll go by my clock and it says they've got five minutes. How about it, Dutton? If you have the money . . ."

"I've got it, but there's some aspects of this case you'd better know, Judge," Ollie said, "and then you'd better send for the sheriff to arrest Bellew for stage robbing. He hired Bronc Killion's gang to hold us up. They were to take the ten thousand dollars I was carrying and then he was to pay 'em another ten thousand dollars for their trouble if they pulled the job off."

"It's a damned lie!" Bellew bellowed.

"They hit us the afternoon after we left Alamosa," Ollie said. "I tricked them into taking a leather bag I was carrying that had some money in it, but not the ten thousand I was bringing from Denver for the Katydid. When we got to the Bear Creek station, the band of renegade Indians that have been raising hell had wiped out all of Killion's bunch except Bronc. He was hit, but he lived long enough to warn us of the Indian ambush. Then he told us the whole deal."

"It's a lie, I tell you!" Bellew raged. "Dutton doesn't have the money, and this is his way of trying to get around it."

"There were enough witnesses who heard what Killion said to make this stand up, Judge," Ollie said. "It isn't enough for Bellew to put the squeeze on Duke and Pete and me, but he had to copper his bet and put everybody on that stage in danger. There were two women among the passengers, and they could have been killed the same as anyone else if there had been a fight."

"Two minutes!" Bellew raged. "Two minutes and you haven't showed us the color of your money."

"Jean Mason has it," Ollie said. "She came back with us from Alamosa."

"Wait," Lorne said. "Duke, you go get the sheriff. He'll want to talk to all of the passengers, but if Dutton's story holds up . . ."

Bellew had moved away from the desk. Now he cried out, the involuntary sound that a man might make when he sees his world dissolving in front of him. He went for his gun, but Ollie, watching him, caught the first hint of the down-ward sweep of his hand as he started his draw.

Ollie brought his gun out of leather and fired, the bullet slamming into Bellew's bull-like body just as he squeezed the trigger. Ollie felt the breath of Bellew's bullet as it snapped past his head. He fired again. Bellew fell back against the wall, his feet slid out from under him, and he sat down hard, his head banging against the wall.

Ollie held his fire then; he saw the shocked, surprised expression on Bellew's face as if the man could not believe he had been defeated. He was bleeding at the mouth and the look of death was on his face. Still, he reached out with his right hand to search on the floor for the gun he had dropped, and then his control was gone, and he spilled over on his side.

Quickly Ollie turned to the door. Jean stood there, the lunch box in her hand. He took it from her and pushed her back out of the doorway. He carried the box to Lorne's desk, took off the lid, and emptied the contents in front of the judge, the dried-out sandwiches and the bundles of money.

"Well, so that's the way you got it through," Lorne said in amazement.

"I'll sign the papers later," Ollie said. "Duke and Pete can sign now. I'll bring the sheriff."

Risley and Warren held out their hands and Ollie shook them, saying: "You boys don't know the half of it. I'll tell you the rest later."

He left the lawyer's office and caught up with Jean who had started toward the sheriff's office. He fell into step beside her as he said: "Maybe our troubles are behind us and we can start doing some of the things we want to . . . like getting married."

She looked up at him and smiled as she slid an arm through his. "Well, I guess we can handle any trouble that comes after what we've been through since we left Alamosa."

"You bet we can," he said.

"Ollie, how would you like a double wedding?" Jean asked. "I thought it would be nice."

"You mean with Johnny and Sally?"

She laughed softly. "No, I don't want to wait that long. Johnny's going to need a little more time. Sally was grateful to him but she's got to do some thinking about it. No, I meant Ida and Mike."

"Sure," Ollie said. "It would be fine."

It was a good world, Ollie thought as he and Jean hurried along Durango's main street, a far better world than he'd had any right to expect a few hours ago.

About the Author

Wayne D. Overholser won three Spur Awards from the Western Writers of America and has a long list of fine Western titles to his credit. He was born in Pomeroy, Washington, and attended the University of Montana, University of Oregon, and the University of Southern California before becoming a public schoolteacher and principal in various Oregon communities. He began writing for Western pulp magazines in 1936 and within a couple of years was a regular contributor to Street & Smith's *Western Story Magazine* and Fiction House's *Lariat Story Magazine*. *Buckaroo's Code* (1947) was his first Western novel and remains one of his best. In the 1950s and 1960s, having retired from academic work to concentrate on writing, he would publish as many as four books a year under his own name or a pseudonym, most prominently as Joseph Wayne. *The Violent Land* (1954), *The Lone Deputy* (1957), *The Bitter Night* (1961), and *Riders of the Sundowns* (1997) are among the finest of the Overholser titles. *The Sweet and Bitter Land* (1950), *Bunch Grass* (1955), and *Land of Promises* (1962) are among the best Joseph Wayne titles, and *Law Man* (1953) is a most rewarding novel under the Lee Leighton pseudonym. Overholser's Western novels, whatever the byline, are based on a solid knowledge of the history and customs of the 19th-century West, particularly when set in his two favorite Western states, Oregon and Colorado. Many of his novels are first-person narratives, a technique that tends to bring an added dimension of vividness to the frontier experiences of his narrators and frequently, as in *Cast a Long Shadow* (1957), the female characters one encounters are among the most memorable. He wrote his numerous novels with a consistent skill and an uncommon sensi-tivity to the depths of human character. Almost invariably, his stories weave a spell of their own with their scenes and images of social and economic forces often in conflict and the diverse ways of life and personalities that made the American Western frontier so unique a time and place in human history.

Center Point Large Print
600 Brooks Road / PO Box 1
Thorndike, ME 04986-0001 USA

(207) 568-3717

US & Canada:
1 800 929-9108
www.centerpointlargeprint.com